A DIFFERENT SEA

CLAUDIO MAGRIS, scholar and critic specializing in the field of German literature and culture, was born in Trieste in 1939. After graduating from the University of Turin, he lectured there in German Language and Literature from 1970 to 1978. He now teaches in the faculty of Literature and Philosophy at the University of Trieste. He is the author of many works of literary criticism and has translated works by Ibsen, Kleist and Schnitzler. His most important work is *Danube*, published in every major European language and generally acknowledged to be a masterpiece; *The Times* remarked that the author is "an acute and inspiring critic" and noted also that "he writes with great beauty and artistry" – as is evident in Patrick Creagh's translation, which won the John Florio prize.

A Different Sea is a winner of the 1992 Palazzo al Bosco prize.

CLAUDIO MAGRIS

A
DIFFERENT
SEA

Translated from the Italian by
M S Spurr

HARVILL
An Imprint of HarperCollins*Publishers*

First published in Italy with the title *Un altro mare*
by Garzanti Editore, Milan, in 1991
First published in Great Britain in 1993
by Harvill,
an imprint of HarperCollins*Publishers*,
77/85 Fulham Palace road,
Hammersmith, London W6 8JB

1 3 5 7 9 10 8 6 4 2

A CIP catalogue record for this book
is available from the British Library.

ISBN 0 00 271339 X

Photoset in Linotron Galliard
Printed in Great Britain by
Hartnolls Limited, Bodmin, Cornwall

To Francesco and Paolo

I

Ἀρετὴ τιμὴν φέρει, virtue brings honour. Or rather, and with greater philological precision, *Tugend bringt Ehre.* Konrad Nussbaumer their teacher, who had been top of his class in his own day, expected the German version. It was only natural in the dingy classrooms of the old Royal Imperial Staatsgymnasium of Gorizia; only natural among those orderly rows of desks as identical as the leaves of the wall calendar that rustled as they disappeared day by day beneath the janitor's hand; and natural too within those walls, whose greyness may simply have been the faded trace of some earlier lost colour.

Perhaps it had begun there when he had entered those classrooms and felt that something was missing. The ink-well on the desk was the deep, dark eye of a cyclops, while the reflected blue of the ink's wavy lines on the glass recalled the distant sea – or even simply the mountains of the Collio, so easy to reach after school. The longing to immerse himself in that blue emptied lessons of meaning.

And, as he waited impatiently for them to finish, how painful, how futile the present seemed. Why was it not already over and done with?

Now, all around him is the sea, nothing but sea. No longer the Adriatic of Pirano and Salvore, where a few months before everything had happened, nor even the Mediterranean, subject to the ancient authority of the aorist and the sequence of tenses, more familiar to him than Italian or even German, but instead the ocean, monotonous and without limit. Big waves in the darkness, a spray of white foam, the wing of a bird plunging into the shadows – standing motionless for hours on deck, he never tires of the unchanging scene. The bow of the ship slices the water without ever seeming to touch it as it falls into the void of the trough opening beneath; the muffled sound of the wave breaks further back against the ship's side.

It is now night, and nothing is visible. But even before, with his eyes half-closed against the relentless sun, with dark red blotches appearing beneath his eyelids, the deep blue of sea and sky had seemed black. After all, the universe itself is dark, and only the eye, like some pedantic philologist, is obsessed with the translation of invisible wavelengths into light and colour. Nothing is really visible, not even in the noon sun's blinding reflection on the shimmering sea. A magical time, when gods appear.

Whether this voyage of escape marks the beginning or end of his life is uncertain. His curriculum vitae reads: Enrico Mreule, born Rubbia 1st June 1886; son of Gregorio (deceased) and Giulia Venier; home address since 1898, Flat

1, no. 3 Via Petrarca, Gorizia; final school examinations taken at the Royal Imperial Gymnasium. And so on. A list of incontrovertible facts, which, perhaps, he can no longer readily list in their entirety – not because he wants to cover his tracks or put anyone off his trail, but because, rising up from that dark, forever resounding sea, comes an overwhelming sense of the utter triviality of all such personal detail. He feels pride, but anonymously. It is not his personal virtue, although in some way it brings him honour, as Nussbaumer liked to put it in their translation classes.

Enrico left for Argentina on 28th November 1909, boarding ship at Trieste. He informed almost no one of his real purpose and told his mother that he needed some money for travel in Greece, to set the seal on his degree in philology at the Universities of Innsbruck and Graz. His father had died many years before, but his family had been able to maintain a certain modest affluence, thanks to some mills in the vicinity of Gorizia. And anyway, money was all his mother was capable of providing to help him on his way.

His younger brother is their mother's favourite. Yet it is not easy for either of them, any more than for their sister, to kiss her bitter, unmaternal face. Enrico feels pity for that mouth, twisted and hardened by the mysterious pain common to all hearts that have difficulty in loving. But his pity is devoid of compassion. There on deck, as he watches the ship's wake being swallowed by the night, Enrico determines to think no more of his mother's face, of their mutual and unpaid debt, of the misunderstandings that have entangled them both. That thought loses itself among the ship's masts and the darkness, loses itself for ever. It is strange how easily and painlessly one can free oneself. And a moment later even his sense of surprise disappears, together with any lingering feelings of remorse. Now he feels merely listless, deafened by the night wind and the sound of the sea.

Only Nino had gone to see him off at Trieste. In the ship's navigation room there must surely be a sextant to chart their position by the height of the stars from the horizon, stars which sink imperceptibly as one travels south. Enrico tries to imagine the sextant and the other navigational instruments that prevent them getting lost, that confirm their position, indeed their identity, on this vast and uniform expanse of water. His life, he muses, whatever happens to him – on either side of the ocean – will always be directed by the trigonometry of that attic room, where each day the three of them – Carlo, he and Nino – used to meet.

When they first got to know each other, at school, Carlo was still listed in the class register as Karl Michelstædter. He immediately became, as Enrico had written to him shortly before sailing, "the friend who would fill all space and embody the world I was searching for". They derived enormous pleasure and a sense of wonderment from their shared view of the world. Up in Nino's attic in Gorizia they would read Homer, the tragedians, the Pre-Socratics, Plato, and the New Testament in the original Greek, and Schopenhauer – also, of course, in the original; the *Vedas*, the *Upanishads*, the Sermon of Benares and the other

4

teachings of Buddha; Ibsen, Leopardi, and Tolstoy. They used to exchange their thoughts and describe the day's events, like that story of Carlo and the dog, in ancient Greek, and then translate them into Latin for fun.

Something had happened in that attic, something both straightforward and definitive – a call, or rather a summons, as clear as the limpid air of those days when they went swimming and skimmed stones in the Isonzo river. A smile from Carlo – a wave's white crest beneath dark eyes and black hair – and off they go, assured, as though leaving the table to step on to the dance floor, or to climb Mount San Valentin – with persuasion.

Nino Paternolli, then, had accompanied him to Trieste from Gorizia – a short journey past rugged rocks and rust-red sumach, the clotted blood of autumn beneath a heavy sky. It was evening when they arrived at the port. Up above, banks of dark cloud shifted apart, and a limp breeze wiped their faces like a cloth. The *Columbia*'s lights lit up a greenish patch of water beneath her bow where a pumpkin bobbed up and down among rinds, peelings and other rubbish, like a swollen breast of a ship's figurehead fallen from some prow and gnawed by the sea.

The ship's lantern threw a cone of light on the water, as did the Florentine lamp on the paper-strewn desk – an oil lamp, with a tall stand and hooked, religious burners, which illuminated Carlo's sheets of paper as he covered them in his large, bold hand. He enjoyed the act of writing. Free and direct as he was, never anxious or fretful, never hurrying to

5

fondle the finished and bound volume, never like an actor eager to perform but impatient of the work involved in producing the play. The lamp still sits on Nino's desk in the attic, its lampshade decorated with phrases from the Pre-Socratics. But the pistol must lie in some drawer. Enrico had wanted to take it with him but it was not permitted on board ship. So he left it with Carlo, the only person with whom he could leave anything.

Carlo had told him that he would go up to the attic window at the moment when the ship was due to weigh anchor and look through the gathering dusk towards Trieste. It was as though his eyes could search out things in the darkness, saving them from obscurity. Carlo had taught him that by virtue of philosophy – the love of seamless wisdom – distant things could be seen close up, and the urge to grasp them could be overcome, since, after all, they exist in the great quietness of being. Who could tell what expression Carlo wore as he leaned out of the window, his dark eyes peering into the night? An ambivalent tinge of sadness, possibly; a bitter longing to prevent this escape which had, perhaps excessively, fired his admiration?

On board that ship now making its way across the Atlantic, is Enrico intent on escape or on arrival? Does he wish that he had already escaped, already lived? He himself is not actually moving. Even those few steps from his cabin to the deck or to the dining room seem out of place in the grand stillness of the sea. The sea remains the same, always at its place around the ship. The ship presumes to furrow it, the water falls away just for a moment and then closes in again. The earth, with a mother's patience, tolerates the plough that gashes, but the sea is a huge, unattainable smile where nothing leaves its mark. Swimmers' arms never embrace it: they only drive it off and then lose it. The sea gives itself to no one.

Carlo had said that. Or rather he had placed it at the beginning of his masterpiece now nearing completion. Maybe the original suggestion for the image had come from Enrico himself or from Nino – without their even noticing it – while out in the boat or lying on the white rocks of Salvore. It is one of those images that flit through the mind and disappear, unless picked up by someone who knows just where to put it to make it shine. Similarly, perhaps, it was a disciple who, without realizing its significance, pointed out to Jesus a lily in the field. He and Nino brought to that attic numerous notes gathered from their own thoughts, from people's expressions, from the yellowing leaves of the horse-chestnuts in Piazza Ginnastica. But it was Carlo alone who knew how to unite them into a ninth symphony.

You know how to exist entirely in the present, Rico, they had said to him as he left. You do not search apprehensively for a harbour when out at sea; you do not devalue your life through fear of losing it. Enrico watches a wet patch dry out on deck. Evaporation is rapid and the moisture-darkened surface becomes steadily lighter as the elements separate out almost visibly. Sweat too dries on the skin. You belong, Rico, on the raging sea. Enrico looks towards the horizon. Those words should make him happy. And they do – to a certain extent. But he stands up and goes for a beer, just for something to do. He has always liked beer, especially the German variety. In his student days at Innsbruck he used to cross the border to drink, since he found the Austrian beer insipid.

Perhaps he did not explain himself properly, even though they talked all night before he left. For a start, he left Gorizia to avoid military service – but not because he is opposed to the Dual Monarchy as are so many of his irredentist friends. On the contrary, he likes the idea of Gorizia as a sort of Habsburg Nice: the image of a retired colonel out for an ever gentler stroll, the two-headed eagle with its wings inadvertently beginning to fold and its eye, scanning the far-flung corners of its empire, a glass button sewn on a stuffed bird. Gorizia's ethnic mixture and its painful struggle had turned it into a great place of learning, of civilization, and of death. It was also a centre for linguistic studies, for death specializes in the pluperfect and the future perfect. The linguist Graziado Isaia Ascoli of Gorizia died in Milan shortly after they left school. Like Manzoni he had been made a Senator. Jews from those parts had always had a weakness for Italy, but Ascoli had realized only too well that it was no use trying to rinse the languages of the multilingual Isonzo in the waters of the Arno or any other river.

Enrico has a gift for languages. He speaks and writes ancient Greek and Latin as well as he does German or even his own dialect. And now on board ship bound for Argentina he is having a go at Spanish too. Federico Simzig, headmaster of the Staatsgymnasium, would count him a true Gorizian. For, to lead a full and satisfying life in his view, you need Italian, German, Slovenian, Friulan, and Trieste-Venetian. Enrico is also fairly fluent in Slovenian, which he picked up as a child playing in the streets at Rubbia. And later on, while swimming in the Isonzo with his friends, when he saw that Carlo and Nino did not understand what Stane Jarc, his class-mate, said to Josip Peternel as he splashed him for fun, he thought to himself how so many things in life remain unheard and undeciphered.

Nussbaumer was right to insist that Greek be translated into German, for they are the two indispensable languages, perhaps the only languages in which birth and death can be discussed. Italian is different. Italian for him is not the language of statements, or of definitions which stun with their brightness or their space. Instead it is the language of postponement, of digression, the language for coming to terms with the unbearable, for keeping destiny at bay for a while by dint of constant chatter. In short, Italian is the language of life, the language of reconciliation, of indebtedness like life itself, or, at most, like a suit – worn to satisfy social convention.

Besides, Enrico's Italian falters every so often, even in letters to his friends. That reminds him, he must write to Carlo, who is doubtless anxious to have his news and to continue their dialogue. Enrico too is eager to communicate. Long and detailed letters from Carlo would surely already be on their way aboard some following ship.

Enrico too has already written. When the *Columbia* docked at Almeria on 3rd December, he had disembarked, bought some writing paper, and settled down in the café nearest the port. He had sat there staring at the white sheet of paper, in front of a glass of thick, rather too syrupy wine, rolling his pen down the slightly sloping table and catching it before it fell. He had wanted to write of his journey, of the advantages and disadvantages of leaving, and of that perilous and unworthy self-love which enslaves one with homesickness. This voyage will be no escape, his departure no form of death. It will on the contrary come to represent life, existence, and an unshakeable stand. It is fear, striving, and ambition that will be routed and disappear.

He had fiddled with his pen, drunk another glass of wine, and undone the top button of his shirt. All things considered, it is only the tight collar of the uniform and, worse, the boots, that make military service unbearable. For Enrico likes to take his shoes off whenever he can; and the thought of having to make up his bunk bed every morning has no appeal. Otherwise he has nothing against the army. He might be incapable of order in his own life, but he recognizes the need for it in the world at large, not excluding the rowdy seamen in this café in Almeria. Even Schopenhauer, whose stern and sarcastic portrait they had propped up against their books in the attic, had accepted the existence of an army and a police force to keep the riff-raff in order, though he personally had renounced all desire for life and power. However, Enrico had never summoned the courage

10

to discuss this subject with Carlo, except in the vaguest terms.

Sitting there in the café, he had continued to doodle on the now crumpled paper. All of a sudden he stopped, threw it away and bought a postcard. He wrote two lines in a bigger hand than usual. "Dear Carlo, things have been too confused over the past week to do more than send this card with my fond greetings. Your friend Enrico."

He will write at greater length when things are quieter, when fewer people pass him by as they stroll along the deck in the long afternoons on the open sea, and when the pace of change slows. In certain moments, as he gazes at the sea, even the colours, changing as the day unfolds, seem too intrusive.

A bigger wave than usual strikes the ship and its spray flashes yellow in a porthole's light. A few months ago at Pirano and Salvore, they did not let out the sheet quickly enough while sailing back against the wind, and the waves, though much smaller than these, swamped the boat. From the beach Paula and Fulvia laughed to see them struggle. They laughed too when Nino threw Enrico in, fed up with him sitting on the water's edge, gazing into the distance while the others were swimming. Then he was forced to swim and, in fact, did so better than the others, with greater force and style, cutting through, or diving beneath, the oncoming waves. Objects seemed to expand in the dark blue stillness which became ever calmer the deeper one dived. And the colours – of the seaweed, the rocks, and the fish that veered slowly this way and that and then disappeared among the *posidonia* – were flashes of light amid the under-water peace.

Paula used to swim down and hold his hand on the seabed, her hair and dark eyelashes like underwater grasses. She had the same eyes and hair as Carlo, and there beneath the waves the resemblance between brother and sister struck him even more. She smiled, and her sweet, ironic smile was still in the unmoving watery veil between them. Then she was away, upwards, with a flick of a foot that shone white like a fish. He watched her disappear. Resurfacing was painful – on the ears too.

Carlo often stayed inside the house by the beach, listen-ing to Argia play the piano. Perhaps he was in love with Argia, in love perhaps with the meaning of her name: "peace", the peace of ceasing from fretful action, from questioning. "Through activity to peace", "through *energia* to *argia*", Carlo had written on the portrait of Schopenhauer – the peace of being, of the sea. Perhaps, Enrico muses for a moment, he means inertia on a bigger scale, the definitive inactivity. However, that is a mistake, a thought unworthy of Carlo, who never demands to exist, as a beggar might, but like a king, simply exists, forever com-plete and fully alive.

Three days spent at Pirano, gazing at the waves from the beach or out in the boat to Salvore on the point of Istria opposite the white lighthouse beyond the white rocks, lying flat and looking over the side almost at the level of the water.

What is low is good. To rise up is presumptuous, the vanity of those who stand on tiptoe to attract attention. The boat heeled over slightly and sailed on unaided. Enrico's face touched the water like a fish rippling the surface. He lay face-down. Paula lay on her back, her head thrust backwards, her dark hair, black in the wind, brushed against his face. Behind her black hair the blue sea shimmered, and beyond lay the strip of red earth and the soft, dark green of cypresses and pines. The underside of a seagull shone ivory as it plummeted and skimmed over the water. An olive tree spread its branches with the stark sexuality of nature. But the boat had already rounded the point, the white lighthouse was in view, the olive's scent already lost on the open sea. The boat glided lightly over the water and vanished in its own reflection, adrift in the afternoon.

In those brief, still days, Enrico had seen the threads of his destiny, had seen the coins of his life thrown up high and glitter for a moment as they turned over in the air. When Argia was not on the beach she was indoors playing the piano. Playing Beethoven for Carlo she revealed the abyss that comes between the individual and his destiny; she annulled time and with it the misery and transience of life, and she demonstrated the tragic joy to be gained by living only for the moment.

The others, meanwhile, were outside, down at the water's edge laughing or silent, doing nothing in particular. Nino was barbecuing fish. Fulvia bounced the beach-ball on the rocks until she tired of it and, with a kick from her tanned

13

and slender foot, sent the ball into the water, to let the waves bring it back to the shore. Fulviargiaula, as the three girls used sometimes to sign their names on postcards, were a single entity, as were he, Carlo and Nino. Fulvia laughed as she splashed them; Argia, her face shaded by her hat, watched a seagull; Paula smiled with her dark eyes, Carlo's eyes, as she poured coffee; a shapely leg dabbled in the water.

They had read Ibsen together. Peer Gynt lost bits of himself along the way but still existed whole and entire in Solvejg's heart. Perhaps Enrico too exists fully only in the hearts of Fulviargiaula, Carlo and Nino. Maybe he has fallen overboard without realizing it, and been lost at sea during the night. No matter. He exists *there*. They often went swimming at night, even when there was no moon. Paula slipped into the water lightly, like a leaf, and taking his hand pulled him after her. Sometimes it was Fulvia or Nino or Carlo, dry and clear, like a rush of joy.

Enrico has never been happier than in those days when he saw Carlo happy, in that mysterious yet familiar sea, so different from the ocean that now surrounds the *Columbia*. This is the *Mare Tenebrarum*, the sea of nothingness, shapeless and bitter, where nothing ever happens. The voyages of Odysseus and of the Argonauts take place in the Mediterranean and the Adriatic, but their legendary tales end at the pillars of Hercules, the edge of the world. At school, Nussbaumer had made them read Apollonius Rhodius and some scholarly dissertations on the disputed route of Jason and his companions. One such was by Carli, *The Expedition of the Argonauts to Colchis. In Four Volumes*, published in 1745, which strove to disprove that Jason had ever passed through the Adriatic via Cherso and Lussino and the Istrian sea – places lying along the route of all odysseys of persuasion.

But there is no place for Fulviargiaula on ships which break through the grey ocean like breakwaters of oblivion. And yet things might have been different a few years ago, according to the *Columbia*'s bosun, a certain Vidulich, with whom Enrico plays *préférence* on evenings when the vast open space and unending twilight seem too empty and motionless even for him.

Forget Cape Horn or the Cape of Good Hope, says Vidulich shuffling the cards, they're so much eyewash. Take it from one who's been rounding them all his life – the real test, God help you, is the Quarnero. Granted, we were in smaller boats in those days, but what difference does that make? Take Captain Petrina from Lussino, or rather from Lussingrande – he used to get really cross if they said he came from Lussinpiccolo! In the *Contessa Hilda* he used to run rings round all those famous English clippers, aye the English ones, that lapped up the ocean like a bowl of milk.

> The sea is vi-olent and the boat is to-ossing
> And you're not the only girl to make love to me

he used to sing to himself on putting out to sea. On graduation, as Providence dictated, from the Nautical Academy of

Lussino, he set off to burrow his way into all the seven seas like a mouse into cheese. For full forty years he rounded your Cape Horns and your Capes of Good Hope as easily as the local ferry captains steer through the shoals of Lussinpiccolo. A ripple or two on the water or the slightest change to the wind's tune in the rigging, and our Captain Aldebrando Petrina could tell at once that a sea was getting up.

Through the porthole Enrico can see the dark and angry water. Wave and spray seem identical, their antiphony incomprehensible. But he likes listening to Vidulich's stories of Atlantic crossings with Petrina, like when they put in at Ascension Island and all those huge birds hauled themselves back into the forest at the ship's approach. Or of their voyages past the Scillies, when Petrina told them to keep their eyes peeled or they'd end up on the long list of shipwrecks. Not that there was any danger between the isles of Tresco and St Mary's, where the flowers and birds evoke the Garden of Eden, where the light-blue water breaks white on the granite sand that shines like gold dust. No, it was on the windward side, out to sea, one of the most damnable points on the globe, where his great-great-grandfather had gone down that Petrina used to make the sign of the cross and swig a bottle to his health beyond the grave. And he never went to sea without his harmonium. Otherwise, he loudly protested, I won't go beyond the breakwater. And if that doesn't suit the owner or the purser, they can find themselves another stooge of a captain – there are plenty of us around.

Enrico plays clubs. He is practised at *préférence*, although he likes Trieste or Treviso cards best, perhaps because the ace of the coin-shaped *danari*, round, sparkling and empty was the highest card. Petrina loved playing music and singing, Vidulich remarks, as he smugly produces his ace. Yes, and popular songs too – "Oh little swallow flying across the sea, stop I want a word with you" – but Verdi and Donizetti were his favourites. He used to round Cape Horn in a pandemonium of wind and wave, towers of water on all sides, sea and sky indistinguishable. Yet he brought the ship round and never missed a beat. "Shit hard and piss strong", he used to mutter as the ship heeled over, and then he would launch into a song in the midst of the screeching elements –

> My ardent sighs will come borne to you on breezes,
> You will hear the echo of my laments in
> the murmuring sea.

Lord, what a character he was! He conducted that whole orchestra of confusion, with a kind word or a joke for every-one – he even threw bits of fish to the petrels swooping overhead. He was not one to take any nonsense from a couple of colliding oceans. If they thought they could mess with someone born and bred on a sea lashed by the *bora* and *tramontana* between Lussino and San Pietro in Nembi, they could think again. And when Petrina came ashore there was singing and dancing in every tavern in the southern hemisphere. He was a real live wire.

Carlo would have enjoyed that voice in the tempest. Repeating over and over the same aria, as calm as anything in the teeth of the storm, singing for the sake of singing. That was it. Just like at Pirano and Salvore. They could have spent their whole life in Captain Petrina's company aboard the *Columbia*, sailing the seven seas and never landing – "my ardent sighs will come borne to you on breezes".

But Captain Petrina had died in 1906. Vidulich remembers the day well. They had just traversed three oceans – the Atlantic, the Indian, and the Pacific, ambling along from Trieste to Chile. A sudden blast from the brass section and he'd dropped dead on deck. The cork popped and the bubbly gushed out – but without fuss. Sooner or later everyone has to meet his maker, Petrina included.

> Die we have to, die we must, bare our arses
> without a fuss.

He was buried at Iquique in Chile, more or less on the outskirts of Lussingrande. Pity he hadn't been able to see his own funeral; he would have liked it: all done nice and proper and everyone snivelling away. He liked a good funeral. Not least because you finished up drinking in some bar.

Too late – that voice had been silenced, although somewhere it must exist still, as a breath scattered to the winds. *Nil de nilo fit et nil in nilum abit*, as Enrico had once jotted down. But he'd never cared for melodrama – too syrupy and, invariably, too loud. He likes the *Lieder* of Beethoven and Schubert, where everyday things become remote – a flower in a glass of water, a tree outside the house. Or if one must indulge in a spot of sentimentality, there's always *La Paloma* – a dove as white as the snow – or perhaps better – as white as the sea – it makes no difference. For the sea turns sparkling white with foam. Sea and snow everywhere are identical. If only everything were identical, like the view on all sides of the ship. Maximilian of Mexico, too, was partial to *La Paloma*.

So Petrina's voice is no more. True, the less we have, the lighter we travel, but it's still a shame. On board ship people travel light, and there is no need to keep on shifting what little baggage one has, as one does on a train. Cabin class may not be luxury, but it is the very impossibility of action, the very leisure imposed by sea travel, which spins out time and then discards it, that is the real privilege. When he has a moment, he will write to Carlo and the others and send the letters in a batch to Peternel: Josip's a true friend, he'll see to their distribution, saving him both effort and money.

The days overlap, merge and then cancel each other out. He sits for hours just gazing at the ship's wake – it disperses more quickly here on these choppy waters than in the Adriatic. He plays cards with Vidulich and Gigetto, a businessman travelling first class whom Enrico had known slightly in Gorizia. Always on the move around the globe, he spends most of his time in Africa, trafficking in God knows what with the Berbers. For him, crossing the Atlantic is like crossing a tributary of the Isonzo. What's more, he is obviously wealthy. Vidulich asks him if it is true that a merchant once, up in the Atlas, made him a gift of a fourteen-year-old slave girl. "I took her out of pity and treated her like a daughter," Gigetto replies, changing the subject. He is a respectable and dapper man. He tells the story of his rescue by an Austrian warship in the bay of Madagascar – his cousin Francesco happened to be serving on board at the time and, rapt in mathematics and philosophy, had tried to explain to Gigetto his key to the universe, while fixing him with the vacant stare typical of a mind on a different plane. Late in the evening, Vidulich stands them a round at the bar, but Enrico is not much of a drinker. In the darkness words become increasingly infrequent, dying like shooting stars.

The ship docks for a day and a half at Las Palmas. Enrico goes ashore, although he would just as happily stay on board and view the city from his deckchair. Soon, however, he begins to enjoy himself wandering through the narrow streets, looking at the shops, listening to the Spanish voices, and scrutinizing the terracotta faces. The racial mixture here is different from that in his small corner of the Danubian Empire. Both poorer and nobler, they bear with indifference their inherited conflict of racial origins. Had these varied peoples never come, had the clear-skinned, auburn-haired Guanches been the island's only denizens, he could have ended his voyage here and now – installed beneath a tree in the garden of the Hesperides, reaching up every so often to pluck a golden apple, letting the sun sink in more western lands.

He picks his way through red crags to the water's edge, removes his shoes, and rolls up his trousers. Now and then a wave splashes over him. He enjoys feeling his shirt dry against his skin in the warm wind. The coal-like sand and pebbles on the black beach gleam in the wash of the waves. Every dark shadow has dignity. In Homer, the waters of Ocean are black. Beyond, the rest of the beach is red, like a frozen sunset. Enrico enters a small cave and picks off the shellfish clinging in the crevices. Tiny sea insects spread over the rock like goose flesh; greenish-yellow crabs scuttle away. Wings rustle in the darkness. A wave penetrates deep within the cave. Out to sea the water shines a metallic blue but on entering the cave turns brown and then black, like ink splashed against the glass sides of an inkwell.

In these caves the Guanches guarded the king's virgins. Here, revered and fattened, they became soft and huge until they attained sufficient imperious opulence to melt their sovereign. Enrico also is not averse to sinking into vast and yielding bosoms. Every body teaches humility, and Enrico is not a choosy type. Love-making is a tasty snack – quick and uncomplicated, enjoyed and then forgotten. One woman is just like another, each with some small defect but all right as a whole – the Majorcan girl, for instance, he met yesterday in a café just after landing who took him to a house of peeling plaster, blue jacaranda flowers at the windows, and a neo-classical courtyard. At Pirano the girls' room had adjoined their own. Yet it was more distant than this house with its small peristyle, where he would never again set foot.

The same girl is available again today. But after only half an hour Enrico does not know what more to do with her. He

21

invents some polite excuse and takes his leave. Wandering along the beach he wonders where it was that centuries ago, according to tradition, two Guanches had found a wooden statue of the Madonna washed up on the shore. They had set it up in a cave where it was revered from time immemorial. Then, one stormy night, the sea had taken it back. Some maintained that the statue was not of the Virgin, but rather a corsair's figurehead in the likeness of a female prisoner who had thrown herself into the sea, so as not to submit to the pirate captain. He had then commissioned a figurehead in her likeness, with her distant, gentle, but unyielding face. And some time later, when his vessel was sunk in battle, he had cast the figurehead into the sea, to prevent it going down with the ship, and the waves had carried it to land. But centuries later she yearned once more for the open seas and had summoned the waves to take her back. Others, however, believed it really had been the Virgin, the star of the sea who, disgusted by the degenerate ways of men, despite centuries of prayer and devotion, had abandoned them for the high seas and the fish. For fish sin less than men.

Both explanations are a little too devoutly Catholic for Enrico's taste. He is more intrigued by the theory that these islands had originally been part of Atlantis. He pauses in front of an ancient *drago* tree, possibly even older than the cult of the Madonna. It was not so much its height that fascinated him as its sideways expansion and tangled branches stretching out seemingly without limit. Any moment now it would collapse under its own excessive growth. Proliferation courts disaster. His Austrian education taught Enrico the virtue of cutting back, of doing less. He learned that lesson once and for all and not only from his teacher of philosophy, of the love of wisdom, who sought demotion not promotion. The trunk and branches are split, wrinkled and streaked with oblique gashes; they sprout hoary beards and bushy eyebrows, obscene protuberances and calloused hands. Wounds open, squinting eyes mock, mountainsides slip and rise up again, ravines slash deep into the valleys, mucus oozes from a coarse cleft, buds and moist shoots rip open the decrepit bark.

With a battered hat on his head and his shirt hanging out of his trousers in the warm December weather, Enrico studies this Silenus tottering beneath the weight of its own vitality, fully expecting a gnarled and over-extended branch to come crashing down. Branches should be pruned. Proliferation is a rhetorical, bubonic swelling to be lanced and cauterized. Shape is achieved by reduction. His teacher, Richard von Schubert-Soldern, a tall, thin man, used to twist a yellow pencil round and round in his fingers as he talked. He would look only at the grey of the walls, never directly at his pupils, and had never been willing to explain his refusal of the Chair of Philosophy at the University of Leipzig. He became a supply teacher at Maribor instead, and later taught history, geography, and philosophy at Enrico's school in Gorizia.

That is the way forward, not the tropical tumescence of this tree. To presume something from life leads to megalomania, as Ibsen said. Even Buddha only started the true life when he ceased to yearn and instead drained the spurting, excess lymph that bloats the heart and glands. Carlo's smile, however, is as fresh as limpid water. Persuasion should resemble drinking, as Carlo drank from the fountain in the school courtyard, without compulsion – either of burning thirst or surfeit. Let the water flow. Don't block up the spring. Right now Enrico would like to dry out that *drago* tree, to drain its veins. Carlo too would dislike such riotous bombastic growth, although in a different way. What his reaction would be, Enrico wasn't sure. He just knew that it would have taken another form.

Standing in front of this tree Enrico now thinks he understands Schubert-Soldern and his notorious decision that amazed everyone and eluded all obvious explanation. Whenever they used to put the question to him directly, Schubert-Soldern would reply politely, with vague and incongruous hints about his health. Occasionally he explained to them in class his own theory of gnoseology and solipsism, contained in capacious tomes held by some library or other, according to which the only knowable reality is the knowledge of the knower. He used punctiliously to distinguish this position from the practical solipsism spitefully attributed to him by certain colleagues. But given his view that life is ruled by mutual misunderstanding, he had no need to worry if his audience was either intellectually incapable or unwilling to understand him.

And right now, back home in Gorizia, Schubert-Soldern would be taking his customary stroll after school along the banks of the Isonzo, watching the river for a while, and then buying two cakes for his wife from a pastry shop in Via Municipio. To reduce, to compact: civilization, like gardening, is the art of pruning. Enrico, however, is disenchanted with civilization. He refused military service not least because he would have had to shave his head. He wants to do his own thing. But something doesn't quite add up. Where does one have to go to become a Schubert-Soldern? Gorizia or Patagonia? Where is it that nothing happens? It will be easier back on board, where the ship's steady rolling aids thought. He will write to Carlo, to Nino, and to Paula, to tell them of this afternoon at Las Palmas and to hear their views.

He lies back on his bunk with relief and stares at the ceiling as he waits for the siren to signal their departure and for sleep to come. The *Columbia* glides through the billowing sea, the sun rises and the stars set, the ship's wake is forever erased. The sextant plots their position, the primeval chaos becomes evermore distant, and, after another two or three ports of call, arrival and departure are indistinguishable.

Enrico writes his first letter, to Carlo naturally, from Neuquen on the Rio Negro, a rough township facing the Andes on the borders of Patagonia. "Just to say hello and to ask you to pass on my good wishes to the family. Affectionately yours, Enrico."

II

There is not much to say about Patagonia. One doesn't go to listen to the sound of the wind in the thorn bushes just for the sake of the odd anecdote. Not Enrico at any rate. Giving others a guided tour of one's life, letting them wonder at its marvels or merely at its curiosities – God forbid! Besides, no one ever stops to listen or really tries to understand. Alien faces the lot of them, like those in that train at Bologna. What does it matter if it was only a dream? As if there was any more life in the harsh faces giving him blank stares in that compartment as he awoke.

No idle chit-chat. Ban poets from the philosopher's Ideal State, and even from the tent pitched for the night. That band of sycophants who worship reality and cultivate personal misfortune, all of them so proud of their petty feelings and their rhyming skills – "Jack Sprat would eat no fat" – one lot winking knowingly, the other lot listening open-mouthed, pretending to understand. Leopardi was different. He was free of self-love and had even ceased resenting his own unhappiness.

On the pampas and afterwards in Patagonia, Enrico gazes at the moon, Leopardi's Nomadic Shepherd, that asks no questions: it is white and chipped, like a piece of chalk. Carlo too jettisons the ballast. He has no time for endless, head-spinning gossip, malicious rumours, intrigues, insolence, tragedies, confusion. In Carlo's poetry there is only the open sea, a sea without shores, and without ships. No Aphrodite jumping out of a shell: life is not a circus.

For a short while Enrico toyed with the idea of teaching at the Dante Alighieri Institute at Bahia Blanca. An Italian from Finale Ligure, a one-time baker, tile-manufacturer, and now successful wine-merchant, tried to persuade him to take up the position, filling Enrico's head with plausible arguments: Italians in Argentina should stick together in the unstable political climate; everyone was envious of them because they knew how to work, as he did too in his own small way; it was an old story that had been going on for years. Pro Menelik graffiti were one thing, but the bands of Acuña, at Cañada de Gomez, were something else – real thugs, with no sense of gratitude for all the Italians of the Legion Valiente did to free their country. The Italians must get organized now and stick together. The best and only focus was the Dante Alighieri Society, he told Enrico, both non-religious and patriotic. After all, it had been the Freemasons who had made Italy, not those sermon-mumblers and miracle-marvellers of the Association for the Support of Catholic Missionaries.

But Enrico understood little of these matters. The Masonic King of Italy interested him no more than the Apostolic

Emperor whom he had refused to serve. He wanted nothing to do with either the anarchist escapees from Italian prisons or the Salesians who had spread as far as San Nicolas de Los Arroyos. Before this he had taken a job delivering horses to some engineers building a railway in the Cordillera. Enrico owned two horses, first-class animals, as fast and as agile as any guanaco or ostrich. After that he had joined up with two Germans and bought a thousand sheep and several hundred head of cattle and horses. They drove them from one cattle station to another, six hundred kilometres north and south, buying and selling on their own account or for a third party. He also went into business with a cousin of his, but it didn't work out. Nothing too disastrous or worth complaining about, as he had written to Nino, given the nature of the business and the people involved.

Seppenhofer, one of his school friends who had gone out there as well, had been unable to cope and had returned home after a few months. Enrico isn't worried. He feels no sadness or remorse. Every wish destroys true existence. One must be free from vain belief in self. Death kills that belief only, nothing or no one else; to depart is to die a little, and is therefore nothing. Enrico copied out in pencil in his blue notebook a phrase he had written as a sixteen-year-old. *Die Freiheit ist im Nichts*: freedom exists in nothingness. Imagine being a schoolmaster. Every bit of knowledge is merely rhetoric – teaching it is even worse.

Instead now he spends all day on horseback, teaching nothing and no one. Occasionally he shouts at the herd to keep it together, but that's all. They are sturdy animals with warm, brown backs rippling like the sea over the limitless plains; their shoulders rise and fall, panting in unison with motherly breath; he among them, on horseback, lost in the hot flush of evening as it fades slowly but unquenchably. The sun sinks red and warm into the dark silhouette of those backs. The moist warmth of their flanks against the hand feels good. Darkness slides like a thin serpent into the heavens, swallowing clouds, sun and sky and then, dilating and swelling python-like, it coils itself in a pool of shadows to blot out everything but the docile gleam of cows' eyes. Enrico dismounts, wraps himself in a blanket on the ground and immediately falls asleep.

Riding gives him pleasure. For one moment, as his boot touches the sweaty flank beneath, he and his horse become one. The erudite centaur, Chiron, had spoken Enrico's preferred language. In Gorizia he rode whenever he had an opportunity. So it was that his romance with Carla began. Beautiful, haughty, impetuous Carla, with eyes so blue beneath chestnut hair. She is his second cousin and her blue eyes resemble his – perhaps they are too alike, if only in their eyes. Dreaming of riding across prairies in the wind Carla waits – either to join him or for his return. She waits, her head high, for the true life that waiting destroys.

When fatigued after hours of riding, Enrico likes to sleep in the saddle. His head resting on his horse's mane and secured to its neck with the reins, he continues to ride, half asleep, just seeing through half-shut eyes. In this distracted state, thoughts flood in – of soft dark waters, of the sea's bed, of the opaque swish of underwater weeds and grass, a cradle of long brown hair. Carla's chestnut hair, Paula's black hair, Fulviargiaula, three tones of tympano rebounding, muffled, sobbing beneath the water. Paula's dark and burning eyes, the phosphorescent night sea of August. Things may be neither good nor evil, Carlo, but such indifference carries its own penalty. A stifled smacking sound sank underwater. Farewell Carlo. I should like to find you here when I wake.

Correspondence is difficult because of the distance and the unreliable poste restante. Some letters addressed to Enrico care of Verzegnassi the chemist in Buenos Aires were sent back again. His mother posted him a cheque without adding a word: he returned it without a reply. Carlo wrote to say that the thought that he would soon have news of Enrico made him feel less miserable. Enrico reads his letter again: "From you we are expecting a most important contribution to our reality." He puts the letter away and looks at his feet resting on a log next to the fire. For once he is wearing socks, as it is cold. Close by, a calf, its muzzle nearly touching the ground, gives him a blank stare. To graze, to ruminate, to die. It is a relief to lighten the load. His talent is for reducing things, not for increasing them. Why do they expect things from him that he cannot give? He gets to his feet and goes for a walk, paying no attention to the animals that shy nervously away.

He writes back and a few months later receives another letter from Carlo, puzzled about his reticence which he attributes to the trials and difficulties that his friend is having to endure "out there". But the fact is that Enrico, "out here", is doing fine and has all he needs. True, he has left his heart in Gorizia with Carlo, but one can survive well enough without a heart – like having an artificial hand or leg. All it takes is a bit of practice and then one can climb again into the saddle without difficulty. The problem lies only in explaining one's feelings.

Carlo's words arrive, large and peremptory, raining down like arrows in the void. "We have been inevitably drawn to you in our grey lives... we have come to understand the meaning of a confident and dignified conscience... you give definition to mankind and the material world... you, Rico, are a being of superior strength, like a saint, serene and assured in whatever circumstances of life or of death... you are showing us the way towards a true valuation of things." Dated 28th November, as he was leaving. A saint in Patagonia? Enrico lifts his eyes from the page to a large, dense cloud in the sky. It is as though it is his body floating away up there, leaving on its own account, while he himself, half reclining on the earth, is merely an empty form, the imprint of something that has been carried off.

Carlo wrote those words to him, Enrico. It should have been the other way round. His heart either contracts or swells. He understands little of these cardiac metaphors, but some part of him somewhere is definitely trembling. It isn't right. Their having been at school together means a great deal – but not everything. One of them is called Carlo, the other Enrico. Were it not for the time he had pointed out that thread of water falling down over the rock, perhaps Carlo would never have written that piece on life, how it flows and then is lost. But you

31

cannot expect someone always to stay on the pedestal you make for him. Nino, too, always feels the need to rush ahead and reach the top of the hill during an otherwise enjoyable walk in the woods, while Enrico is happy enough lying on the grass and watching the daisies grow.

29th June 1910: "You, Rico, with your self-assurance, live your life ready for anything. Everything, whatever the peril, has a way of turning spontaneously to you. Because you ask for nothing. It is as though you do not notice the passage of time for, by acting in every moment, you are free of it. Thus too every word you utter derives from a life of freedom..." Carlo is right, Enrico asks for nothing. He does not even ask why and how it is that everything just seems to come his way – this letter, for instance, which is even, perhaps, too much.

When he is out riding, with that rush of excitement that brings colour to his cheeks, his troubled thoughts are forgotten. Sometimes after hours in the saddle he grows thirsty. So he lassos a wild horse and then slackens the rope, leaving the animal to lead him to some tiny spring it knows among the rocks with threads of cold, silent rust. At other times he has to kill a horse and drink its blood to quench his thirst.

He moves a little further south, towards San Carlos de Bariloche. He spends all day and every day in the saddle, careful to keep the herds from straying and getting lost. As soon as he can he will build a large corral, worry less about the animals escaping, and not wake up before they stir at dawn in the cold wind that comes, passing over few living things on its way, from the frozen distant wastes. But obtaining timber and building an enclosure are expensive, and right now he has no money. He must be patient and wait.

Wagon trains come past every so often. Enrico sells an animal and buys some tobacco, rice, biscuits, and coffee. Occasionally there are women travelling south with the wagons and then back up north, with a view to meeting men of his sort. One can afford to sleep with them for three days on the proceeds from the sale of a horse or calf, if the wagon trains stop that long; otherwise an hour is good enough. The women are fine mounts with strong flanks that know how to carry a good weight. And when minded they can show a bit of unexpected spirit that takes one by surprise. Yet whenever Enrico thinks about them, he can never conjure up any single one in all her particulars. He never remembers which face goes with which oversized breasts or with which gargantuan rump. There was one woman who, immediately it was over, would pull some flat maize bread and lard from her poncho and begin to eat, while he was still caressing her back, thinking it nicer to wind down slowly and not to have it over and done with all at once.

Occasionally too he sleeps with Indian women, but only rarely. He is stimulated by their harsh, closed faces, something which makes him feel rather ashamed. With them he rushes in like a nervous boy rather than relaxing and enjoying himself like a man. They twist like snakes and mutter incomprehensibly, while with the other women there is an amiable understanding that a poor devil doesn't have to make an effort to satisfy them. You and she understand and tolerate each other, whereas the Indian woman beneath him is beyond reach. Perhaps she is

33

enjoying it but, if so, it is without noticing him. He might as well not exist: it is as though he simply isn't there. Only his pestle grinding away on its own account.

But it doesn't happen very often. People pass by so rarely. He admires the way the Indian women give birth without fuss. As soon as it is over they get to their feet and, if it's winter, break the ice of the frozen stream to wash themselves and the baby. If the child is healthy the cold does no harm, and if it dies – well it would not have survived anyway. Enrico doesn't stop to think about it, not least because he has never been able to endure babies, especially when they scream. The Indians he respects. But then the Indians respect each other. They harm nothing, neither man nor beast, without good reason. They strip life to the bone, like a leg of guanaco. His teacher Schubert-Soldern is an Indian too in his way. At times they defecate like horses, upright, with regal nonchalance, in their rapid stride across the prairie.

He has built himself a cabin, but just to sleep in, with a plank of wood for a bed. When hungry, he kills a sheep or shoots a rabbit. He has a good aim, and is in general capable and accurate – with horses as with the Greek aorist. Basic skill is only proper, since everything has the right to be treated with due care. It is right to know how to pick a flower without damaging it. To roast a piece of meat one only needs two stones and some firewood. And when it is months since the last wagon train, and he has run out of salt, he does not waste his meat. Instead he chews it, tasteless though it is, without spoiling it by wishing for the salt he lacks.

34

The milk too is good. He drinks it warm, straight from the bucket beneath the cow. He removes his sombrero to scoop out some milk – much easier than drinking from cupped hands. There is no need to lock up his cabin. It's enough to wedge the door with a stone to keep out the rain and the animals. From the Cordillera to the coast there is talk of outlaws, of Butch Cassidy, the Sundance Kid, or Evans, dead or resurrected. But no one ever passes by his way – for the past two years he hasn't seen a soul. He has no need of a lock on the door to protect two planks of wood, a couple of blankets, and five or six Teubner classical texts.

Enrico detests locks, as he does ties. But that does not mean that others could rifle through his kit. Absolutely not. In fact the letter from Tolstoy annoyed him for that reason. The grand old man replied magnanimously and irrevocably to him, an unknown lad from Gorizia, and he kept those four sheets written in German, along with the letters from Carlo, among the pages of Sophocles. Enrico had written to Tolstoy – from the attic, of course. That was where they had read the works of Ibsen and Tolstoy. Those two Atlases who propped up the world had shaken it to its foundations by sundering themselves inexorably from the rhetoric in which they, like all the rest, had their roots. Truth was enshrined in their writing, as in the music of Beethoven. Enrico had written with reckless candour: he had wanted to become a follower, to enter the commune. The grand old man's reply had been brusque and majestic: he could come but first he should give all that he owned to the poor, as is written in the Gospels. It was easy enough for Tolstoy to give away his wife's possessions, but that did not go down at all well

35

with Enrico. Better Schopenhauer, who kept a close watch on his purse and his food. Enrico prefers to own nothing, to undress on the banks of the Isonzo, to strip naked and throw himself into the water. But why should someone come along and carry off his rags and get praise for it? It is a senseless, empty gesture, as when his uncle Giuseppe gave away his townhouse in Gradisca and then sponged off his brothers.

No, Enrico has no time either for Socialists or Christians in catacombs. A Buddhist monk with his begging bowl and no shoes is all right; after all, it's nice to go around with bare feet. But those communes with their hearts on their sleeves must really be the limit, each more intrusive and irritating than the last. What is certain is that they make a great noise about it. What a crazy idea, living squashed altogether and sticking their noses into each others' affairs. Thank God he realized in time, and is now in Patagonia, not Jasnaja Poljana after helping a few layabouts.

Admittedly it can be seen as a fine gesture, a real act of largesse – and yet that other gesture, of replying to an impudent boy, is also great, perhaps even as fine as the one the old man expected of him. Sell off everything and give the money to the poor. Is that the true life? Why is it that everyone expects the impossible of him? Better Ibsen, who did not suffer from megalomania. And yet it is true to say Enrico never thinks of his father's mills in Gorizia, nor knows anything of his share of the inheritance or even how much money his family has.

Every so often the horses get sick with a fever that affects their lungs. He knows what to do. He opens a vein with his knife at the right place and bleeds it. Then he makes the horses gulp down *ginebra* or, if that doesn't do the trick, the whisky he bought off a Welshman, until they get drunk. Their heads droop with lolling tongues and rolling eyes, but then after a few days they recover. Once he finds himself face to face with a puma. His horse shies, and when he whips it furiously and even bites it, it throws and tramples him. For months afterward he pisses blood, until some Indians cure him with a decoction from the bark of certain trees.

He goes to Bahia Blanca for the big cattle fair. Thousands of animals are herded in from all over the country, and the earth pounded by their hooves is as slimy as grape pulp after the wine-making. The big traders are already there waiting and paying out money in huge wads.

There are prostitutes too from every corner of the country. For forty-eight hours money floods through the hands of the cattlemen, like the blackberries they used to cram into their mouths by the handful on the wooded slopes of San Valentin, bursting and crushing them with their teeth, careless of the juice running down their chins. Indian women, half-castes, negro girls with big red bows – all crowding round his horse like cows on the prairie, shouting and waving, with flashing eyes and white teeth. As evening comes on, a flask of wine breaks across the sky, spreading everywhere, even to the flushed and excited faces of the crowd.

The cattlemen throw bags of money into the hands raised and reaching towards them. Enrico does the same, not only for the sake of a barefoot girl with dark braided hair, but also for the sheer happiness of tossing something away, like throwing stones into the Isonzo and making them skip on the surface of the water. All around him is shouting, laughter, the lowing of cattle, the cracking of whips, fireworks going off, pomegranates erupting, their scarlet seeds spraying out into the night sky. With the girl in his saddle he loses himself for a while in the deafening jamboree. But he has soon had as much as he can take of the shouts, the lights, and the crush, and sets off for home. After a few days on the trail he reaches his cabin, moves the rock aside, and lies down to sleep.

He does not reckon up the days and the weeks. Instead he uses more elastic, indeterminate ways of measuring time – the first flurry of sleet, the grass's loss of colour, the rutting of the guanacos. There is always a wind, and after a while one learns to distinguish its different moods, from hour to hour and from season to season, a tugging, drawn-out whistle, a dry rasp like a cough. At times the wind seems coloured – golden brown in the scrub, black on the desolate plain.

Large clouds float by and are gone, a cow tugs free a clump of grass, the earth turns yet also stands still, a daisy lasts a month, a mayfly just one day, the evening star is the morning star. Sometimes the sky opens out like a sphere of blown glass, grows distant and vanishes.

Enrico fires. The wild duck plummets to the ground, one moment in heraldic flight, the next a piece of rubbish tossed from a window. The law of gravity makes nature clumsy. Only words are protected – such as those printed in the Teubner Greek and Latin texts from Leipzig.

The shot's echo dies out among the rocks. Carlo shot himself with Enrico's pistol. The final curtain has been lowered. There is nothing more to say – for Enrico that is, not for Carlo, over whom that instantaneous gesture can have no power, just as the cerebral haemorrhage has no power over Ibsen, or pneumonia over Tolstoy, or hemlock over Socrates. Carlo is the conscience of his age. Death has power only over the verb "to have" not over the verb "to be". Enrico has his herds, his horse, and a few books.

He learned of Carlo's death a year after it happened, in the September of 1911. The news was waiting for him on his arrival at Puerto Madryn on the coast after a journey of six hundred kilometres. Nino had written to tell him and had enclosed a copy of the poems Carlo had written since Enrico's departure, in the last year of his life. "I have had the good fortune, denied you, of being close to him, of seeing him, of sharing his life right to the end. Now we are alike, and his death binds us even more closely. What he taught me, you have learned in a different way by yourself. How life seemed then and how it seems now! All that is over, for ever. No life, no joy will ever equal that for which I believed I only had to wait."

The rope that binds us also drags us down, thinks Enrico. Carlo did not miss his footing that 17th day of October 1910. No, Carlo is completing the ascent and disappearing on high like a swallow. It is he and Nino who are slipping on a treacherous slope. In his major work, *Persuasion and Rhetoric*, written in their attic, Carlo states that a weight can only descend or fall. Now Nino's words weigh on Enrico's shoulders. "Carlo spoke of you and looked to your life as one entirely worthy of esteem... you put his teachings into practice, in every single action of your daily life. For you it is not just a question of having knowledge... those close to Carlo think of you as his natural successor."

Enrico looks at his saddle, at his shoes that pinch his feet, and at the receipts he has come to cash. If only he had found letters from Nino and Peternel accusing him, as on previous occasions, of reticence, lack of feeling, and of mockery. Such criticisms might be refuted or ignored at will. He flicks through the pages of Carlo's *Dialogue on Health*, completed on 7th October, ten days before his death, which Nino had copied out. "What is inscribed here – Nino had added – is the ultimate expression of the written word." Would it not have been better if they had stayed as they once were in that attic, all together just talking, without any of them, not even Carlo, writing a word?

The slim dialogue sweeps him along like a wind. Occasionally it clutches at him, and he gasps for air. After drawing a deep breath he scans the pages and notices his own name time and time again. He is the protagonist of the piece – the part of truth, of resolute affirmation, of persuasion, of condemnation of suicide as fear of life and death. In those intense pages Enrico represents the truly free man, of whom it is said "you are", who enjoys life simply because he exists, demanding and fearing nothing, neither life nor death, fully and always alive – in every instant, including the last.

Enrico roasts some duck and watches what little smoke there is disperse. For a few moments he is happy, but with a happiness that comes and goes. When it goes, the sky lowers, sluggish and

40

heavy. He tries to recite the words and phrases of the Rico in the dialogue, to hear how they sound. Why hadn't Carlo reversed the roles, with Nino taking the leading part and he the one who listens and learns? Of course he recognizes himself in the protagonist's ability to shun the cicada-like chatterers, slaves of a swarming society who flatter themselves with the pretence that they are free. Enrico does not waste his life by attempting to seize it, nor does he destroy his shadow by turning round to look at it. This at least is one lesson he has learned. Carlo can rest assured. The sun can do whatever it wishes with his shadow – lengthen it, shorten it, even distort it – for all he cares. He plans to let his shadow fend for itself, even to vanish when the sun goes into hiding.

But why Rico and not Nino? A light burns within him, Carlo's lamp was extinguished not because the oil ran out but because its wick flooded. He too has an internal flame, but outwardly it splutters unsteadily – flaring up on occasion, but then soon dying down again. The heart beats in the dark, a bird enters the cave where, blinded by the sunlight, it loses its way in the blackness, striking its wings against razor-sharp walls.

The pages lie on the ground. He places a stone on top of them to prevent their blowing away. Perhaps they ought to disappear in the wind. This mandate from the blue contains a misunderstanding that cannot now be put right. Out here death counts for something. Although powerless over truth, it is nevertheless the inescapable judge of all misunderstandings and misinterpretations. Men do not grieve because of death, Carlo said, they die because of grief.

He studies the diagram Carlo has drawn to illustrate the text. It consists of four intersecting circles producing sectors in common. To the left, or west as it were, of the circle of happiness, lies the sector of freedom, of "no-need". Yes, it is here in this white space that Enrico is to be found. But the defining arc sweeps on downwards to form another circle, in the south of the diagram – the circle of death. "No-need" – freedom – appears in both circles: in that of happiness, founded on being and value, which needs nothing – because it exists; and in that of death, which likewise needs nothing – because it does not exist.

Enrico looks at the curving horizon, the moving but identifiable edge of the herd, the bit of ground which, although roofed over with planks of wood, belongs as much to the open prairie as to the enclosed space of his cabin. Boundaries on all sides both separate and unite so many different things. Perhaps Carlo is wrong: Enrico is at a boundary, as in Gorizia, yet without knowing on which side – or in which circle – he stands. Is he on the south-eastern frontier of happiness, or on death's north-western border? When walking in the woods in the direction of Friuli they often lost their way, without knowing whether or not they had already crossed the border into Italy. Carlo is now telling him to return, to belong in freedom to the luminous circle – the circle of happiness and of being. Or, rather, he is ordering him to guide the others, to lead them in his name to the other side.

The investiture both stuns and inebriates him. It also weighs him down, for it is too much – a misunderstanding that strikes him like a stone. He must sort things out, lift this bright but heavy star from his shoulders before it crushes him, and return home to the attic. Why didn't he sort it all out long before, when there was so much more time? It is impossible now – it is simply too late. No effort can defeat death. Due to death's cowardice the record can never be put straight. Everyone dies before clarifying something or other. Thus killing is a crime. He regrets shooting that duck flying so fast and straight – perhaps on its way to put something to rights.

But if Carlo wishes it thus, Enrico will retrace his steps, change circles, and climb up towards the ray of freedom, to the silence enjoyed by the one who is free of all desire, up to the tops of trees warmed in the red of the sunset. Climb that tree aflame with the sun's rays and flee the evening shadow scaling its trunk. The sky above is the burning light of fire, yet Enrico would prefer to turn and look down at the grass round the base of the tree as it loses its colour in the darkness, to stretch out on the ground below, to sink into the damp turf and then, from that position, to watch the sky gradually drain of colour.

Carlo should understand that his request, or rather gift, is too much. Even he used to laugh when Enrico recited his favourite poem, a nonsense-rhyme of Panarces: "a man who is a non-man, seeing and not seeing a bird that is a non-bird, perched in a tree that is a non-tree, hits it and does not hit it with a stone that is a non-stone..."

Non, non, dong, dong, the sound of bells. The flesh of the duck is good, although unsalted. He finishes it with care. He likes eating well. Besides, it is manly. Among the gauchos he who eats the most is the most virile. He goes to his cabin, pulls out a Teubner text and sits in the doorway. The moon is bright enough to read by, but he can easily manage without it – he knows those heavily underlined passages by heart. For the first time ever, he feels condemned rather than comforted by Plato's view that it is to thought that the magnificence and the vision of all time and all being are revealed. For nothing is revealed on that stark plateau. This does not worry him too much, but it is not good enough for Carlo, who wants him really to see that magnificence.

Enrico looks around, a lump in his throat. He puts away *The Republic* and reads in turn the *Electra*, *Oedipus the King*, and the chorus of the *Orestes*. "O Night, queen and giver of sleep, rise up from Erebus on your wings, come, we are lost, swallowed in darkness." He just wants to go to sleep, nothing more, even simply to doze like the animals scattered in the darkness still diluted with light, like coffee with milk.

He finds himself in this state only once in a while – his soul agitated by a drawn-out dusk, a wild night in his cabin with moonlight filtering between the planks. Such moods are rare. Generally life drags by with empty identical days and months, the years passing or not passing, as in Panarces' rhyme. To keep in practice he revises *Sprechen Sie Attisch?*, a conversation guide to ancient Greek, and repeats phrases of every day use: wie lebt es sich in Leipzig?: τίς ἔσθ' ὁ ἐν Λειψία βίος? I have a headache: ἀλγῶ τὴν κεφαλήν. He is also reading *Martin Fierro*. He likes the world it evokes, without childhood, where

44

death and murder are unimportant, simply because dying and killing are accepted practice.

He recalls a story once told him by a gaucho as they sat round a camp fire. Was it one year ago or three? No matter. The gaucho too was no different from any other and played the guitar as they all did. The story concerned a *rastreador* of the pampas of earlier times, an infallible tracker who could recognize and distinguish every print of man or beast even when the trail was weeks old, pounded by hooves, or criss-crossed by wagon-wheels. They used to hire him to track down a lost bullock, a thief, or an outlaw in hiding. Sooner or later, as surely as night follows day, he found his animal or his man.

The years passed. The *rastreador* was now a king of the prairie. But he grew sorrowful and restless and would speak or cry out in fitful sleep. Sometimes he would get up and walk about while still asleep, frightening the horses, but without being woken by their whinnying. One day they called him to search for an unknown person who had murdered a cattle trader. He found the trail and followed it. It was short but involved, twisting back and forth, criss-crossing, and superimposed. Gradually, though, he unravelled it. In the process a great weariness overtook him, for he was old, and it was time he stopped this continual hunt for someone else. But habit and honour and something else compelled him to persevere. He stuck to it like a bloodhound and finally arrived before his own four-plank cabin with torn curtains. Only then did he realize that the tracks were his: the only tracks he had never learned. He must have committed the murder in his sleep on one of those troubled nights. Both conquered and conqueror, he handed himself over to the police.

The true version of the story, according to others, was that the old man had murdered from greed, and that another, younger and more skilful tracker had uncovered the trail that he had tried, in vain, to conceal. But the gaucho singing in the shadows that night, when the hot wind dried the mouth, would not admit the existence of anyone more skilled. He alone could bring defeat and destruction on himself. Enrico contemplates his own trail from their attic to his cabin, losing himself for a moment on the journey. It is easy enough to put grief on the wrong track and to conceal his footprints from others, but not from himself. His trail is clear, solitary, both behind and in front, leading on inexorably, ever since Carlo first mapped it out. He gazes at the moon rising among the tall black grass, wanting to discard it like a useless old gourd. But there is no rubbish pit.

The tale of the *rastreador* is an ancient one, with its origins on the shores of another sea that gave birth to the gods and to all stories. Enrico opens *Oedipus the King*, the Berlin edition of 1865 – text by Nauck and commentary by Schneidewin – its scribbled annotations dating from their time in the attic. In a note on line 1400, the commentator observes that the manuscript reading τοὐμόν must result from scribal error, and he suggests an emendation. Enrico takes out his pencil and scribbles an angry comment: "Mierdita, es ist wunderschön richtig – it makes perfect sense!" He stands up, relieved, and goes out to stretch his legs. Anger in the cause of philology is not unenjoyable. The deserted plateau around him is once again as it should be.

Life has its pressures, but it can sometimes prove generous as well. It may even stop to take a rest instead of always forcing us to do something. Enrico was astounded when Mario appeared. Mario had followed his trail with real skill – across an ocean, no mere stream – a hunt well beyond the capacity of an ordinary bloodhound. He looks just like Carla, his sister – the same high forehead, soft but bold eyes, and rebellious mouth. Enrico watches him emerge, utterly unexpected, from the distance, with Carla's sky-blue eyes. What we love is not any individual man or woman, he thinks to himself, but a look, the sea within, a smile transcending gender. It is almost laughable – Mario made this whole journey just to relay a message from Carla. Since Enrico never wrote, no one in Gorizia knew his precise whereabouts, and so Carla sent Mario to say that she still loves him but – how could she put it? – in a somewhat different way. Now she wants to marry someone else but would do so only with his consent, for she had pledged herself to him when he left for South America.

But one doesn't laugh or sneer at someone who traverses the ocean. Horses are at pasture on all sides. Carla loves horses and was made to race before the wind. All he did was fire her imagination in Piazza Ginnastica after school with his talk of riding on the open prairies. It is not that she didn't follow him – thank God she didn't – but rather it is he, Enrico, who is incapable of following her, as she goes forward fearlessly to face life. For unlike the women of the wagon trains, or even, perhaps,

Fulviargiaula, Carla is the child-bearing type; and Enrico can't stand children.

Mario is embarrassed at first. Enrico removes his sombrero and lets the wind riffle his hair. Carla's gaze in Mario's eyes goes straight to his heart. Then he feels relieved, as light as air. It is a splendid day, and he takes Mario off trout fishing. They sit for hours, smoking and watching the water, as every so often a fish struggles on the hook.

The outside world often impinges noisily. America is in uproar, he writes to Nino, even though the huge distances of the prairies muffle the din before it filters through to him. The army of President Yrigoyen fires on the *chilotes* on strike against the *estancia* owners, and continues shooting even though they surrender on condition that their lives are spared. News reaches him of firing squads, mass graves, torture and murder in the prisons. Once, in the centre of Buenos Aires, he himself witnesses the police open fire on an unarmed crowd and then step up the firing with relish as they stampede, trampling the bodies of the dead and wounded.

Even before this massacre the city is in a frightful state, with overcrowding, poor housing, and deafening noise. Everything is in utter confusion, as though a crowd were in continuous flight from spraying bullets. Enrico is now in Buenos Aires with scurvy. There was plenty of meat in his cabin but no fruit and vegetables. Better to be a cow or a sheep and feed on grass. Sores appear on his skin, his gums bleed and his cheeks are scabrous.

As soon as he is cured he flees the noise of Buenos Aires, back to Patagonia. He really must build that corral, get organized,

48

and grow some vegetables. He suffers a relapse, his bones ache too much to stay all day in the saddle. The idea of returning to Buenos Aires, however, appals him. He cannot go on. This chapter of his life is over, and it is best not to dwell on it – just like anything else. He will return to Gorizia. As the ship draws alongside the pier at Trieste, Enrico looks at the shore and, leaning over the side, casts the few remaining pesos from his pockets into the sea.

III

His return to Gorizia in 1922, wearing the new clothes his brother made him buy from Beltrame immediately on landing at Trieste, is not so different from those journeys the length and breadth of Patagonia, where the only folk one met belonged to wagon trains going the other way. There, as paths crossed and in the very moment of exchanging greetings, one was already bidding farewell.

The old Imperial Staatsgymnasium has been renamed Liceo Vittorio Emanuele III, and Schubert-Soldern has left to live as a foreign resident in Austria. Having lost two empires, now that Gorizia is Italian and his native Prague is part of Czechoslovakia, he is reluctant to choose a new identity. Just possibly too he is not discontent with life in the draughty vacuum created by the cyclones and anticyclones of history. He is even able to eke out an existence on a salary arranged by some ingenious bureaucrat of the little new-born state – at least until "his worries ceased" – to use one of his own favourite expressions – on 19th October 1924.

Enrico's arrival coincides with the departure of others. His mother died in 1917 at Udine. Nino dies on 19th August 1923. He falls while climbing and lies trapped for hours in the Houcnik Gorge in Val Tribussa up on Mount Poldanovetz. Carlo was wrong. It is Nino who knew how to live a life of persuasion, with no hankering after romantic escapism or any other such foolishness. His was the great-hearted life, lived in love for his wife Pina and their two daughters, lived for his friends, and in the pleasure he took in his bookshop in Piazza Grande. "He used to regard mankind with nobility," says Marin, one of his friends. Lying there in the coffin, his face shines with the light of their lamp.

Ervino Pocar, who saw him fall, leaves for Milan. He too learned, after a long, devoted and highly successful study of ancient Greek at his desk in their old school, that virtue brings honour. Ervino understood, in the company of his classmates, that to love means to listen, and that reading is more important than writing. Or, as Nussbaumer taught them, if it is really necessary to take up one's pen, translation is best. Placing oneself at the service of the great authors is worthier than self-advertisement. Biagio Marin teaches at a secondary school, and when the authorities decide to transfer him, after taking issue with his teaching of St John's Gospel, he retorts that he is not a piece of luggage, throws it all up and takes himself off to Grado. Others leave as well: Camisi to Egypt, Segalla for the Trentino.

Enrico is confused. It seems that he has left rather than returned, and is again among the gauchos. When last seen, Felipe Gutierrez was heading for the Cordillera, while José

Antonio Pinto was way down south. He spends little time looking at the Carso or the Isonzo, for both have drunk too much blood, as some swamps in South America drink light. And he listens uneasily as his friends speak of their involvement in massacres or attacks and bloody counter-attacks on captured positions.

Enrico notices another aspect of this tragic war in which his friends were set each against each other, but does not try to understand. He says nothing when they speak of a drink of water given to a wounded man under fire, of a soldier who threatened to shoot his own comrades, brutalized from weeks in the trenches, to prevent them butchering a prisoner. He thinks back with unease to Tolstoy's letter and rudely leaves the room. Once he even makes a tart comment about the widow of Walter, one of their friends killed on Mount Sabotino. Then he grows irritable, possibly because he is ashamed, but also to make them leave him in peace. Their fraternity and their pious feelings for the enemy are nothing to him. He has no interest in the enemy, in brothers, or in children. Carlo alone might have been a brother.

Monsignor Fogar, their religious teacher at school, is now Bishop of Trieste and is doing his best to protect the Slavs from fascist terrorism and violence. The Slavs retreat behind an impenetrable wall, making Enrico feel rather in awe of them, although he smarts at the injustices they are suffering. For his boyhood Slovenian, sufficient for friendly games after school at Rubbia or Gorizia, is now like some dead language – inadequate to bridge the gap.

They used to call him "the prof" even on the pampas, and now he takes a teaching job on a yearly contract. A friend, Don Igino Valdemarin, who was also in Carlo's class, is now head of a seminary and uses his influence to help him, despite the fact that Enrico is not a Party member. Don Igino is a poet, aware that a class is a communion of souls as indissoluble and as varied as the communion of the Creed. Each morning at the seminary Enrico listens, with bowed head but without crossing himself or moving his lips, as his pupils pray. He then tests their knowledge of conjugations and declensions. But he never discusses the historical or literary value of a text or talks of Achilles' tears or Ulysses' yearning for his distant homeland.

Doubtless they find him dry, but he is not going to put on an act to win them over. He doesn't approve of seduction. At most he might seduce a woman, but only for as long as it takes: he would never try to win her heart. Even less does he want disciples hanging on his every word and traipsing around behind him, or worse still, following in his footsteps to Patagonia. Adopted children are even more tiresome than one's own. He can't abide the class looking at him as he teaches.

However, no one can complain of dereliction of duty. He teaches according to the rules – Gandino's *Grammatica*, the *Ausführliche Griechische Grammatik* by August Matthild, Leipzig 1835, and the *Repetitorium der lateinischen Syntax und Stilistik* by Menge – books that have crossed the ocean both ways. And he prepares his lessons and the composition exercises with meticulous care. On the back of the *De Bello Gallico*, for example, he has noted that there were ten cohorts to a legion –

the kind of detail he could never remember. After all, he left the country to avoid military service, and he is fed up with hearing about the Great War. What do they expect of him, sitting there at their desks? Let them learn the aorist tense: that is already more than enough.

In Patagonia he kept in his pocket both the *Odyssey* and the *Agamemnon* edited, with commentary in Latin, by Simon Karsten. But a discourse on the fate of the sons of Atreus, or on the suffering of Electra – Carlo liked her best of all – would be out of place in front of these boys. It would be a total farce, like interrupting the paradigm of an irregular verb to gaze out of the window in admiration of the Julian Alps. And anyway, he would only end up making some anti-religious remark in passing, which would be a fine way of thanking those priests for taking him in, and might also give rise to a spot of bother.

He glances at the mountains. It would be nice to be able to point them out to the boys. People who know how to sing while shaving are fortunate. But in class he keeps to the rules. His pupils once drew a caricature on the blackboard of a gaucho on horseback lassoing a weighty Greek lexicon. "What did he say when he came into the classroom and saw it? – Nothing. He looked straight at the blackboard but said nothing."

He exchanges an occasional word in the staff-room with Ceccutti, the only other lay teacher among all the cassocks. He is a good chap and friendly with it. He is always behind or in a hurry and often arrives late without having done his marking. So Enrico gives him a hand in the break between classes – it is no problem for him to spot an error in Greek or Latin. If only

Ceccutti would stop killing himself with all that extra private teaching to support his wife and three children, he could correct those exercises in plenty of time and relax a little. A really likeable character, despite being tired and drawn, who can share a good joke and make even Enrico laugh. He always has some story up his sleeve, making his home life sound even more exciting than Patagonia.

Every so often Ceccutti turns the talk to politics. He is angry with the fascist bully-boys who gave one of his cousins the castor-oil treatment. But worse, in his opinion, are the big estate owners and top civil servants who give the fascists financial support without dirtying their own hands. Enrico agrees, although the κοινωνία κακῶν, the consortium of evil, comes as no surprise to him: both Carlo and Plato always warned him of it. Ceccutti mentions a couple of names, well-known ones apparently, that appear regularly in the newspapers. But they mean nothing to Enrico. He might have seen one of them, perhaps, while passing some farm or factory, but he could not be sure. A person cannot keep abreast of everything.

One evening Ceccutti invites him home for dinner. The house is small, and one armchair has the bottom knocked out of it. Marco, their elder son, had used it as a chariot in a re-enactment of the Trojan war and Giorgio, his brother, ran it through with his broom-handle spear. On the wall can be seen a faded "Long live Giovanna" that the boys painted in red for their sister's birthday, and which their mother has not been able yet completely to clean off. Their habit of all speaking at once during the meal annoys Enrico. Yet he is more tolerant than usual and on

55

his way home he goes for a long walk through the deserted streets, before finally climbing the silent stairs to his flat.

Enrico also gives private lessons – for exorbitant fees. If they can't afford it, then that's their affair. After all, no one is obliged to learn Greek – the fewer the better in Enrico's view. He uses the banknotes as bookmarks, forgetting them among the pages. He is reading the *Cratylus* and the *Theaetetus* in the Teubner edition – a present, with a dedication, from Carlo – and, at the same time, both editions of *Persuasion and Rhetoric*, the first edited by their friend in Florence, Vladimiro Arangio-Ruiz, and published in 1913, the second brought out in 1922 by Carlo's cousin Emilio. He has known that book ever since it started life as Carlo's degree thesis in Florence. The ivory-coloured cover is edged in a deep black, at times resembling the blue-black of night, with a wave pattern picked out in a lighter hue. Between those covers is the definitive statement, the diagnosis of the sickness eating away at mankind.

Persuasion, in Carlo's words, signifies the full ownership, both in and for the present, of one's self and one's life. It is the capacity to live each moment fully, without sacrificing it to what is still to come, to something one hopes is just around the corner, thus destroying life by wishing away the present. But civilization is precisely the history of men incapable of living with persuasion. Instead they construct an enormous barrier – rhetoric, society's way of organizing knowledge and thought – to hide from themselves the reality of their own emptiness. Enrico runs his finger over the border's wavy crest, looks through the book, and makes notes in Italian and German – in the margins, at the foot of the page, and even between the lines. It is best to write nothing. But if it becomes necessary to express oneself in writing, such pencilled comments are the least offensive and rhetorical method.

Only a person of stature, such as Carlo, can write a book; not someone like Enrico. Those two short stories he did once churn out are utter rubbish – a romance set in an imaginary medieval Gorizia and an even feebler one located in the Semmering. Not to mention his really pitiable tales of Indians and bear hunters: there is no need to go and live among real Indians to realize what nonsense they are. But at least such attempts convinced him to give up. Once he even commits one of his dreams to paper – how two old women rob him while he stands in some street in Gorizia dressed only in underpants. The Caffè Commercio too comes into it at some point. The very banality of dreams reflects on psychologists and all those others *quia nesciunt, quae nesciunt, sibi scire videntur.*

Enrico also thumbs through the pages of the 1922 issue of *Convegno*, which includes some pieces written by and about Carlo. He makes a few jottings in the margin – lightly, so that they can be easily rubbed out. At whom or at what were those dark eyes smiling? Life, Enrico scribbles in the margin, is not an enjoyable "good", but pain does cause suffering. It is desire and yearning that consume existence. "Do not project yourself into the future", he writes on page 362: projection into the future = death. Concentrate on the present, awaken from the mad, destructive dream of longing. Carlo, like Buddha, is the great awoken one.

57

The evening descends on Gorizia, the narrow streets disappear in a bruise-grey haze, the wind blows rubbish against the pavement. Enrico detests this dry, biting winter darkness, so different from that darkness they used to watch from the attic, as it settled over the city, soft and empty, like a shell held to the ear. Perhaps it is necessary to eradicate not only the vanity of success but, indeed, every single wish – even that longing for good that was once visible in those dark and smiling eyes; to eradicate even the need of values, since every need harries and pursues the present with fiery breath... Why is it up to him to unravel these knots? He is afraid of heights. His idea of happiness is to lie stretched out on the ground, roll a cigarette and smoke it, gazing at the sea. No, not the sea. It too throws up large concerns – the promise of happiness and the search for meaning, which, in the end, like all searches, suffocates happiness. Better the earth, solid beneath the feet.

It was wrong of Carlo. He ought never to have allowed Enrico a glimpse of something both beyond his reach and almost impossible to live without. Enrico opens the same year's issue of *Ronda*, runs through the pages dedicated to Carlo, commenting hurriedly: "total renunciation that knowingly refuses to participate in any value-system." But who knows whether desire is conquered by this intellectual approach or only by dull, brutish pain? Death resembles too closely the very renunciation needed to conquer it. Enrico has no fear of death, only fear of fearing it, of succumbing one day to the dread of dying.

He goes out into the street. When, every so often, a car passes, he opens the umbrella he invariably carries, to shield his eyes from the glare of the headlights. There are too many cars, too many blinding lights, and too many car horns – Gorizia has become one big noise. People even greet him in the street, as though they're all part of one big family – it's sickening. Let them laugh at his umbrella, perhaps then they won't keep on buttonholing him, and will come to realize from the burning sensation in their eyes that light damages the sight and causes conjunctivitis. You have to keep on your toes and watch your back.

He goes to visit Lini. It's not a serious affair – at least not for him. Perhaps it is for her. Often, deep down, women care more. Love for them is like water for fish: once it's taken away they writhe all over the place, gulping for air. On the other hand, women can't be trusted, since they can play some pretty nasty tricks. The fact is they have to stay in the sea, while men just go for a dip as often as it suits them, get out and shake themselves dry. After all, nature has fitted women for reproduction. They have to deal with all those effluents, bulges, pregnant tums, suckling, pap, dribble, potties, wee-wees, wailing – with no chance to open a book.

Lini, or rather Carolina, is a tall washed-out blonde with an ungainly body and wild, restless, even beautiful, eyes. She says little, asks no questions, is happy when Enrico calls in and even happier when he talks of Carlo. She listens attentively without pretending to understand everything. What does the word "understand" mean anyway? And when he changes the subject, she does not press him. He tires quickly, since women, except for Fulviargiaula, have no gift for philosophy.

Lini gets up, slides her big feet into slippers, and goes into the kitchen to make some coffee. Enrico stays stretched out on the hard bed – he has removed the mattress – and listens to her bustling around with cups and saucers. She doesn't step into the future – just from one room to the other – and every so often a spoon falls to the floor. They do not say much to each other. Sometimes she gets upset about a recent act of fascist violence, but Enrico says nothing: he's reluctant to waste words on what he despises. So they sit at the table in silence. Enrico feels her gaze but avoids it. Then Lini clears away with thin and nervous hands.

Lini scarcely comes into his plans for a trip to the Galapagos Islands, even though she would be happy enough to go. The men will make the decisions – he and Janes. Dr Janes is a friend. He too has read Schopenhauer and agrees that it's wrong to keep the show going for an indefinite run. Living it up is one thing, procreation another. He does have a conscience, though, and once went to the bother of tracking down some girl he had met on holiday, for fear he had got her pregnant. He was prepared to assume responsibility – even for the unwanted child. Forward planning, he used to say, is the thing, adding that it was one of his strengths. As it turned out, he was lucky that time too: the girl wasn't pregnant. She was, however, amazed to see him, since usually in such cases the man is never heard of again. But Dr Janes' hostility to reproduction does not include people who are already alive.

It would be marvellous to go to the Galapagos Islands. Completely deserted, and thus better than Patagonia, just sand, hot seething mud, clumps of grass, giant lizards and tortoises. They will take a couple of women along – they shouldn't be hard to find. Then with the Pacific Ocean all around them, immense and admitting no return, they will watch the evening sun sink into the infinite waters to the west, towards other islands even more remote.

But the Galapagos Islands are for the moment distant. So he and Janes sail along the coast of Istria as far as Pola. Colours absolute, platonic, white stone, red earth, turquoise water flecked in the depths with indigo blue, transparency of the purely present. They drop anchor, swim to shore and stretch out on the rocks or beneath the olive trees. Keeping out to sea they pass Rovigno and the Cathedral of Sant' Eufemia perched on the cliff-top.

At Salvore on the tip of Istria he recognizes the white lighthouse, the avenue of figs and olives, the pines filled with blackbirds, the line of sentinel cypresses, the laurel and the chicory's blue flowers. A boat rocks to and fro below the lighthouse, the sea slapping gently against its side. Chicory's flowers are blue. Yes, but how long do they last? Perhaps the plant itself lives on while the flower falls – to be reborn later, like hair. If so, the fall is not a fall, and this is the same blue flower that dark-eyed Paula disturbed, as she lay in the grass and nudged its stalk with her knee while gazing at the sky. The stones of the beach covered and uncovered by the tide's continuous cycle are still there, white and polished, shining in both sun and water.

This was Carlo's favourite place, he writes to Gaetano Chiavacci, their other great Florentine friend. Who knows if

Arangio-Ruiz and Chiavacci, who are making a profound study of *Persuasion and Rhetoric*, can ever really understand it without having this reflection in their eyes? A stone falls in the water and ripples spread in ever-widening circles until they eventually disappear or, more precisely, become invisible to our feeble sight. Somewhere they continue to exist. So it is that the sea is ruffled, perhaps even beyond the pillars of Hercules, by Argia diving from that rock over there. Neither do voices die. Paula's words have now reached the pines across the bay, and her smile is caught there among the branches and the black-birds' nests. Every so often he encounters Paula: how obvious it all is and how impossible. Even her mouth resembles Carlo's.

The Pensione Predonzani is only a step from the lighthouse. Mulberries and false acacias hide its wrought-iron balcony and ancient well. Enrico knocks at the door to ask for a room. He is barefoot, and his face, shaded by his sombrero, is still scarred from scurvy. Signora Predonzani takes him for a beggar, and her daughter, Anita, gestures to her from behind his back not to take him in. But after a few moments Enrico's blue eyes, so blue and so clear, and his fair, tousled hair, like a halo in the breeze, work their charm – on Signora Predonzani and, even more so, on her daughter. Enrico settles in immediately. Everything is to his liking – all except for the softness of the bed, which he resolves simply by putting the mattress on the floor.

The summers are long and still, with incessant chatter of cicadas and passing hours the colour of amber. As soon as the term ends in Gorizia, Enrico boards the steamer for Salvore.

Disembarking, he discards his shoes near a bollard on the harbour jetty and finds them there again on his departure two months later. He brings with him a few books and a couple of shirts, but leaves his umbrella in Gorizia – with the traffic. The Pensione is comfortable, and geraniums sparkle in the window boxes. Even the other guests are tolerable, especially those from Graz. For the Austrian heart, longing to escape the oppressive Danubian hinterland and to gaze on the open sea, is seized with nostalgia for Trieste and Istria.

The Mayor of Graz, a lawyer, a couple of civil servants, and their wives – pretty if over-talkative – make up the company. When in a good mood, Enrico takes charge and teaches them hand-ball. He makes them jog round the garden in single file to get fit. They puff and pant, but the Mayor, laughing boisterously, enters into the spirit of things and forces the others to touch their toes and vault the low hedges – "so… so und so, hahaha." Enrico instructs Signora Predonzani to reduce the size of the helpings, to put less salt in the seasoning, and not to serve a pudding – even if the Austrians complain that they miss their *cuguluf* and meringue, to say nothing of their Sacher Torte. If they continue stuffing themselves, they will die from heart failure or lose their wits, for salt thickens the arteries and fat dulls the brain. It is crazy to poison oneself with such trash, especially here, where there are so few cars and there's a chance of staying healthy. Foodstore owners are the real scoundrels.

But so be it. After all – the planet is already over-populated and all people can think about is having children: *Il Duce* even rewards them for it. This trend will lead nature to rebel and drive mankind to destruction. Sooner or later we will lose both our sight and hearing, become as blind as bats and as deaf as doorposts, all as a result of believing that we need something extra, like salt in soup, and then slaving away to acquire it. To reduce one's needs, to be happy in oneself, yes – that's the solution. "Well, he doesn't look happy to me," Lidia, Signora Predonzani's niece, remarked in his hearing to a teacher from Trieste. But what could that child know? Happiness has nothing to do with words: either you have it or you don't.

He condescends to talk about Patagonia only when they really beg him. Collecting his thoughts for a moment he begins to speak, with inspired mien and furrowed brow, softly clicking his tongue. The ocean breakers boom like big guns against the islets off the coast of Desolation. Battalions of birds of prey the size of geese plunge from the craggy heights, the *guanayes* screech deafeningly. Whales beach on the rocks, their gaping maws big enough to swallow boats; throngs of scarlet-headed vultures flap into the air and obscure the sky. Patagonian hunters club to death condors gorged, till incapable of flight, on sheep carcasses left as bait. Guanaco they capture by enmeshing their legs with *boleadoras*. Araucanian Indians, with strangely gleaming eyes, are quite untameable.

The ladies listen, giggling, as he describes the Indian women. But no one is more amazed than he to hear the passion and excitement in his voice. All this has nothing to do with his cabin, his horses, or his cows. He is telling stories about things he has never seen and never experienced, just read about in novels – by Salgari and Karl May. He never even went as far south

64

as the tip of Patagonia. But he has no choice. Words can only echo words, not life itself. And his life has been colourless, like water. Yet, just occasionally, one must try to be good company.

He boasts that he discovered an oil field which he left untapped and unpublicized, to keep the world a cleaner place. It lies somewhere near Los Césares, that mysterious city of gold and diamonds, unlocatable among the deserts and ravines of Patagonia, whose last chief was the Indian rebel Gabriel Condorcanquí, Tupac Amaru II. He likes the city's imperial-sounding name, gold ringing hollow with empty words, and is only sad that there is no connection with the ancient Caesars, as one legend has it, but was named instead after Francisco César, a common sailor.

Yet it was there, on a crumbling and rusty rock face, that the Spanish sun had set. The legend of Los Césares had grown up around Puerto de la Hambre, the city of hunger, squalor and solitude. It had been founded for the glory of Philip II of Spain by Pedro de Sarmiento, who had later reached the Magellan Strait afloat on two planks of wood, battered by the confluence of oceans, wounded, delirious with fever, and hounded by Drake like a wolf by dogs. This last Spaniard from Puerto de la Hambre was finally taken on board the English vessel *Delight*, after six years in his empty city surrounded by corpses rotting in their cabins, a silent church, a scaffold rising towards heaven, and pearls strewn about by colonists who knew they would never return home.

That shattered and wretched imperial greatness deserved the name "Caesars" and the mystery of the lost city of gold. The oil field was regal too, since he left it hidden and forgotten. But the City of the Caesars among the mountains had not only never existed, even its name was pure chance, mere coincidence. The foot turns over the shell and exposes the hollowness and silence within.

Myth means story, but myths are silent. From a distance we seem to hear their voices narrating fabulous stories, but as we approach they fade away. Perhaps after all it was just the wind among the ancient stones, and now even that wind has died. But philologists prattle on, expounding those lost stories and their silences. A commentary on a myth is the fiction of its own inexistence, padded with waffle. And Enrico dislikes fiction, Tolstoy excepted, as so much chit-chat for dinner parties, not worth reading and certainly not worth writing.

Women, especially, egg him on to invent such bragging tales. And he yields to them – at least for as long as his blue eyes and winning manner prove attractive. But he soon tires. He needs no one, not even women, although if they really insist then he lets things take their course willingly enough. Like with Inge, the long-legged Austrian journalist with the greedy mouth; or soft Violetta, capricious as the moon, from a family of Triestine industrialists, who makes him appreciate, surprisingly, some of rhetoric's empty concerns – silk stockings, elegant shoes, a scented foulard.

Enrico discovers he has a talent for avoiding relationships that can trap a man like a fly on flypaper. In fact he never has a "relationship", nor even knows the meaning of the word. He sleeps with an Inge or a Violetta for one or two summers, but casually almost, with no fuss and no strings attached. He doesn't even need to break it off. It is they, who, sooner or later, let him go, sadly perhaps, but without anguished reprisals. He tries dutifully to show some regret when it's over, but then, feeling lighter than before, off he goes out in his boat all day long, silent and at peace.

He names his boat *Maia*, a small ten-footer, just big enough to venture out to sea with its white sail – the veil of *Maia*. The haze shimmering in air and on water on certain afternoons is either the final veil drawn over the pure present of things, or is already perhaps in itself, pure present. The sail glides over the sea, slips through a cleft in the horizon, and falls into a milky blue bound by no shore. Summers open out and solidify. Time rounds out like blown glass in water.

He occasionally talks to Lini about Carlo, but never to those other women. Even that is not really a relationship: Lini just happens to be there. In '31 a killer 'flu, known as "pneumonic plague", strikes down his brother Carlo, their mother's favourite; he had survived the war, both as an Austrian soldier up on Mount Podgora, and later on the Italian side, on Mount Sabotino. He dies at Gorizia. Shortly afterwards his sister Ortensia dies too. Enrico, who nursed her, takes to his bed immediately after the funeral with a raging fever. He is at Lini's place, but she is unafraid of contagion.

They give up all hope, even Janes. But Enrico knows what he must do: the horse-cure he used in Patagonia. He lets almost all of his blood drain out. What a relief to feel so much of one-self flow away, so much of that surplus infected waste. Then he stupefies himself with *grappa* until he loses consciousness and understands nothing more beyond gulping from the bottle every now and then. A few days later he can again make out the colour of the wall and focus on the table and the chairs. The weakness he still feels is now mild and benign.

Lini keeps people away. But one day an old lady moves her firmly aside with the words "I am Carlo's mother", and enters the room. Those dark eyes, Carlo's, Paula's – that crease around the mouth... On her way out she places a tall Florentine lamp on his bedside table, the lamp with two hook-shaped burners. It was Carlo's lamp, the one that flooded with oil and went out. She leaves, and Lini, who goes to show her out, catches sight of Enrico propped up on his pillows gazing at the lamp.

IV

On 21st September 1933 Enrico transfers his place of residence
from Gorizia to Umago in Istria. This change, recorded in the
municipal archives, is one of the few irrefutable proofs of his
existence. For there are no records of his flight to Argentina,
where the memory of places and the sequence of events fade,
making it difficult for him to reconstruct his time there with
any precision. The registry records, however, are clear. Umago,
of course, means Salvore, which is one of the areas under its
administrative control.

There are a number of entries of interest in the civil and land
records at this time. In 1934 Enrico marries the beautiful Anita
Predonzani, who is now the postmistress at Salvore. She had
always been drawn to him, and expects to be able to use her
charm and gentle insistence to domesticate him a little. Emma
Luzzatto Michelstaedter, Carlo's mother, congratulates them,
praising the suitability of the marriage in general and of the
bride in particular, even if, as she says, "I still can't get used to
the idea of Mreule as a husband." Paula too is married – to a

69

Swiss called Winteler. It is strange to think of her with someone else's name.

Enrico purchases four hectares from the Benedetti family: olives, a few vines, some fruit trees, and the pines along the shore where he, Carlo, Nino and Fulviargiaula spent that evening in August 1909. He brings with him from Gorizia some of the roughest and most worm-eaten pieces of furniture that had been stored in the cellar, and a supply of old clothes so that he would never need to buy any more. There are no clocks in the house, only a sundial attached to the grey exterior wall. Two chairs next to the bed are more than enough for laying out one's clothes before going to sleep; pleasure comes from being independent of whatever is not absolute – although one should remain indifferent even to necessities. "Nacktes, kahles Selbst," he writes in his blue notebook, the Self naked and stripped, peace of the will, not even a breath of wind in the heart.

No electric light, not even a radio. Anita finds him tougher than predicted. Not even the moments between the sheets are of much use in softening his ways. Carlo's oil lamp is good enough to read by at night. He keeps his books either in a large studded trunk or else under the mattress. When in bed, propped on his pillows, he just feels with his hand and pulls them out. He does not need to look, for he knows the position of each book by heart – the discourses of Buddha or Carlo's poetry – and in the darkness his hand is never more than five centimetres out. His favourite poem is *To Senia*: "Of what I have seen on the floor of the sea, I want you alone, Senia, my listener to be."

70

Because Anita works at the post office, Enrico often does the cooking – a *sbrodaus*, a thick soup, that lasts three days. But on reheating, it often burns, sticks to the bottom and tastes of smoke – because he forgets about it on the wood-fired stove which he stokes with pine cones, collected nearby, that explode in the flames. He cultivates tobacco and makes his own short, stubby cigarettes. If visitors arrive, he escapes to the beach. Dr Janes, who also has a house by the sea, but a little nearer Trieste at Valdoltra, pays them regular visits. The three of them spend happy hours discussing and dreaming of travel. Yet Enrico himself never journeys even as far as Bassanìa, barely a kilometre away, where there is a good little restaurant. And when Anita and Janes insist, he lets them go off by themselves and stays behind, smoking and gazing at the sea beyond the pines.

The evening is a time of changing colour. It is interesting to focus on the individual breaks in the continuum, on the very moments of colour change, without ever lifting one's gaze. From the instant the sun touches that pine over there to the instant it disappears, there are four or perhaps five shifts of colour. The penultimate is the most remarkable: for a moment or two it reverses the process of fading luminosity and, from an almost black, blue-green backcloth, a coin of burning copper emerges, rolls over and vanishes behind a greying curtain.

Afterwards he strolls as far as Pensione Gamboz or the Pensione owned by Captain Pelizzon on the other side of the cove. Or he chats for a while with Captain Cipolla a little further round. But he grows tired quickly. "Dearest Gaetano – he writes to Chiavacci – it is difficult for us, to whom destiny

71

granted the privilege of friendship with Carlo, to be content with that of others."

He re-reads Buddha, the discourses of the last days in which the sublime passes beyond the ultimate limits of perception to the dissolution of the perceptible. He also reads the *Regulations Concerning Share-cropping in the Province of Istria*, and highlights the clauses that concern him most. Clause 7: "The tenant must abstain from carrying out work, transport, or the performance of any other manual services, or services involving the animals of the farm, for third parties." Clause 10: "The tenant may raise poultry in numbers not exceeding three birds for every member of his family, excluding the chicks necessary for renewing the brood. He may raise a pig for fattening for the exclusive needs of his family."

Enrico does in fact have tenants: a Signor Busdachin, his wife, and – unfortunately – two small children. If they produce a third child, he will send them packing, as he has already warned them fair and square. As for the two already in existence, if they make a noise either in the house or outside, there will be trouble. Their parents will have to teach them not to whine and not to run around in the fields or in the wood. Signor Busdachin is a capable sort, much the same as any other man. But his wife is different. Her steady placid eyes, somewhat narrowed by the wrinkles of her peasant skin, look knowingly at Enrico as though they could read in his face more than he could in hers. She is a woman of broad hips and strong arms – fine arms that sow, reap, cook, polish, wash – Enrico's clothes as well – solid arms that carry the pitcher of the present.

The Busdachin woman's gaze exudes goodness, a goodness at once mocking and maternal. Law and order are necessary evils, however. This is no longer Nino's attic – the world outside is harsh. But for these hateful laws there would be all sorts of trouble. Enrico despises them but observes them to the letter. Who knows how things might end up otherwise – if, for example, one were to abandon oneself to the smiling eyes of the woman with the child in her arms?

But she too must learn, she and that stupid child of hers – and the other one that screams even louder. Let them all learn to their cost, as he has, that there is no such thing as living, that no one lives. Let them realize that there is never anything to lose, not even those extra hens he has forced them to get rid of according to the rules. Only when one has understood that, is one free. Only slaves talk idly of rights; the free man has duties.

The stipulations must be rigorously observed, with all their implications of renunciation. Enrico fears neither man nor puma, nor the darkening *bora* that can crash down on a boat at sea. Yet the clauses and sub-clauses of a contract scare him witless. The law states that the tenant is to work the land he leases and share the produce equally with the owner. He is the owner and it is his duty to ensure the law's fulfilment. It is not right, for example, for the children to pluck and eat the occasional piece of fruit from the tree, for that apple or that bunch of grapes does not feature in the final accounts.

He makes sure that the two children keep their hands to themselves. They are mad on figs, but the figs are his. He did not create the world. Indeed, he is of one mind with Buddha, with no wish for life and no yearning. Nevertheless, in the meantime, no one is going to eye his figs let alone touch them. Sometimes Enrico even rifles through the rubbish: a core or piece of peel means an illegal appropriation of his property. It will be the worse for them, and it is no good the Busdachin woman looking at him that way as he searches through the filth. On sheets of paper taken from his notepad he lists all incomings, outgoings, and provisions : to Tita (a cousin of Anna who works at the Pensione) 500; tenant's expenses for grain 66; plough 70; kitchen expenses 50.

Anita soon leaves him for Dr Janes, who, despite the Galapagos project, has running water and electricity in his house. "Now what?" Enrico asks the Busdachin woman. Yet he is neither upset nor surprised. We are all strangers: no passing can cause pain, not even the final one – and least of all that of a woman who walks out of your life. He sharpens a stick, without caring whether the knife-blade loses its edge.

It had been over between him and Anita for some time. She was always complaining about their austere lifestyle and was full of fancy ideas. She thought only of luxuries, obsessed with desire for a radio and heating. Any pretext was good enough for a trip to town – Trieste – without bothering to let him know when she would be back. And that evening she had started yawning repeatedly on purpose and asking him when the steamer left for Trieste in the morning. Although knowing perfectly well how he detested timetables and clocks, she asked him two, even three, times – "right at the very moment of climax during the love-making that she herself had started" – as Enrico wrote in his diary.

That questioning had a paralysing effect on him, as, perhaps, Anita had intended. The night noises came in at the window, and suddenly he was drained of desire. Something beneath his skin and behind his eyes simply dried out; his body lay inert and shrivelled, a stranger to the whole affair. This was not death but non-being. Desire's ultimate deception is to make one believe in it, to expect it, to want it. That night deception ceased. Truth halts things. Consciousness extinguishes desire, and death extinguishes consciousness. He re-reads the *Philoctetes*, as he had in Patagonia. He is the only true hero, whose sore prevents him from being like the others.

But he has no hard feelings, even if Anita did it on purpose. To hate her he needed a greater unthinking faith in himself and his own paltry deeds and triumphs. If he is angry with anyone, it's Janes. But even that's rather half-hearted – anger just for form's sake. In such circumstances there is no need to kill one-self like the gangsters of Buenos Aires. But equally one cannot pretend that nothing has happened, and a friend who acts like Janes is as good as dead. A pity though, for he is a good doctor. And Enrico, who is frightened of illness even though he wanders around in mid-winter in shirt-sleeves and bare feet, would like to be able to call him when necessary.

But now what? In Patagonia solitude is all right, but not here. Here it's too eccentric. To disappear from view one has to be like everyone else – and live with a woman. A man on his own sticks out like a sore thumb. So he goes to Gorizia, to fetch Lini. Or rather, he makes her think that she has succeeded in trapping him. For he allows her to beg him to let her stay at Salvore, and when she comes he mistreats her and locks her out all night – it isn't that cold – while he sleeps peacefully within.

Lini sells her flat in Gorizia and moves in to the house at Salvore with its unplastered walls and exposed beams. Her only two possessions are a clock and a small battery-operated radio that she listens to locked away upstairs out of Enrico's hearing.

From March to November they eat outside, resting their plates and the coffee pot on an upturned fruit crate. Enrico sits on a box, Lini on a proper chair, chain-smoking. His old jackets from Gorizia are of good material. Only their colour fades here and there between patches, like the sky growing softer and clearer as time passes. Lini prepares the food, and gives him a call when it's ready. Or, if he is out at sea, she lights a fire of damp wood and sends smoke signals.

Occasionally Lini goes sailing with him but, more often, she stays at home. The days are long, and she has developed a liking for *pelinkovec* – by eleven she has usually downed several glasses. Some days, glancing at the clock that Enrico pretends not to see, she realizes all of a sudden that it's already gone three. So she puts the hands back to twelve, makes the lunch and calls Enrico. He comes ashore, ties up and flings his entire catch on to the beach for the children to take – all except for a couple of fish that he grills for himself and Lini over pine cones and charcoal.

Enrico grows ever more wiry, his face withers and wrinkles, his hair as always is too long. Lini's arms too are scrawny. He often asks her to read to him as he listens with half-closed eyes, leaning against a tree. She selects from the last days of Buddha, skipping the sections spoken by Ananda, the favourite disciple, because disciples irritate Enrico, or from Carlo's works – some pages from *Persuasion and Rhetoric*, some poetry – "What do you want from the perfidious sea?", but never from the *Dialogue on Health*. She also reads a story by Björnson, in German, of silent waters and fair-haired women.

Although Lini has no love of books, she treats them with cautious respect. Even in those moments when she's doing her hair, she is aware that the life that matters, the life that endures, Enrico's life, is to be found there, in those books. But there is one book she can't stand, *Die Kameradschaftsehe*, by Lindsay and Evans. Presumably the authors are man and wife, or at any rate a man and a woman, but they show precious little under-standing of certain things. Although, Lord knows, their idea of "marriage as friendship" doesn't seem that bad and maybe even has its good points – when Enrico loses his temper and shoves her out of bed because she contradicts him, or when he catches her staring at an aeroplane and throws down a bucket of water to stop her gawping at such deafening contraptions.

On some afternoons when her tongue's clogged with *pelinkovec*, Lini doesn't feel like reading. Instead she complains to Enrico about the Busdachin children's screaming that gave her a headache while he was out at sea. Later on Enrico shouts at the tenant, he in turn takes it out on his wife who, not being able to slap the mistress – that dried-up old bag who goes round acting the lady – belts her two children instead. Then

77

she picks up the stuff that Lini always leaves lying around – it's all in a day's work.

On some Sundays, Tita and Lidia Predonzani come over, with Captain Pelizzon and Captain Cipolla. If they are the only visitors, Enrico does not slip away but stays for a game of cards – *briscola* or *cotecio* – and to listen to them setting the world to rights. Someone says that *Il Duce* is off his rocker. Enrico listens, cheerfully, his head cocked to one side. He lifts a finger, clicks his tongue, and gravely interjects: "Quite so, right, well done." The Slavs are no longer enough for the fascists, they have started their dirty tricks on the Jews as well. Enrico thinks of the dark, eastern eyes of Carlo and Paula. Once Paula comes to visit him – with her son, whose name, of course, is Carlo. And when she leaves, Enrico stays for a long time looking out to sea, his back turned on the others, including Lini, who is busily putting away the plates and glasses.

Even at Salvore, perhaps without realizing it, they cannot escape the Empire proclaimed by *Il Duce*. *Quia non sumus esse volumus et quia esse volumus non sumus*. Not that Enrico has any liking for communists. Communism is a load of nonsense: all it does is give the Slavs big ideas and make them forget hundreds of years of history. Yet it's the communists that keep the fascists on their toes – one has to grant them that. And they don't fear death or even the fear of death, nor do they ask any favours of life, bankrupt as it is. Nevertheless, it will go to the dogs, communism, even in Russia. It must be a nightmare there, all those groups and collectives – a consortium of evil – a sleep from which they will have to awake. Every belief is no more than a dream, and soon turns into a nightmare. One of Cipolla's friends with republican sympathies has gone to fight in Spain. Around the table, or rather the fruit crate, the others speak of him admiringly. Enrico says nothing and gets to his feet for a walk by the sea.

Times are difficult. Although they have very few needs, prices keep rising. Enrico gives an acquaintance in Gorizia power of attorney to sell his flat at Monfalcone, and he keeps a detailed record of all expenses. He enjoys visits from Lia, his brother's daughter: she likes the bare house and the wind gusting in the pines and whipping up the waves. They walk along the beach and among the rocks and caves. He points out the fleshy red sea anemones that open like flower buds when covered at high tide, and together they collect worms for bait.

They also go out in his boat. She is handy with the sheets and bursts into peals of laughter when the *Maia* seems on the point of striking the rocks but suddenly goes about and heads away from the shore. Her laughter is clear, immediate. There's no pain in watching it, as there used to be when he had Fulviargiaula on board.

Lia resembles her father. Looking at her, Enrico sometimes regrets that he and his brother had so little to say to each other. If only they had played more as children, they might have had some good times. On the way back, Lia dives overboard and swims to the shore, then runs off still dripping wet to light the barbecue to grill the fish. Rejecting the broken pine cones, she orders Enrico to go to find some others – whole, big ones – and he enjoys obeying her wishes.

Occasionally, too, they go swimming together, and he lets her grab him by the shoulders and push him under. Perhaps after all Carlo and Paula – discounting the masses that are to be avoided like flies – are not the only people in the world. Enrico even bothers to learn Lia's tastes and is careful to take the fish from the flame before it browns all over – for she likes it a little underdone and garnished with a sprig of rosemary. Lia devours the fish with relish, tossing her hair and throwing her head back. True – this is no illumination of Buddha beneath the tree, but Enrico is happy all the same. As far as he's concerned, she can stay on: it's proving a good season, and he'll ensure that she has plenty of fish grilled to taste.

But the summer is sultry, and the blue sky soon hazes over. When Lia's mother comes to collect her, Enrico tells her bluntly that his brother was irresponsible in producing children who are nobodies and who will never have a penny to their name now he's dead. He goes on to pick a quarrel with her over a medal he wants back, a medal with the bust of Franz Josef – a worthless bauble; it was his father's, he shouts, and so belongs to him not his brother, and he's not about to let himself be cheated by some prattling female who's no longer part of the family.

Carla's daughter, Lisetta, comes to see him once – a loving, adventurous girl just like her mother. Like her mother, too, she loves horses. Enrico talks to her of red Indians and ponies, and they act out some of Karl May's stories, with him as old Shatterhand and her as Chief Winnetou. Thankfully she is not his daughter – not only does that make things so much simpler, it also means that he can more easily bear to see her leave – for Germany, never to return.

He often gets letters from Signora Emma, who is now eighty; "the senseless eighties", as she puts it. In one letter she describes her eightieth birthday party at Gorizia, how she sat at home all day long, from nine in the morning to eleven at night, receiving a never-ending stream of letters, telegrams and flowers – "all worthy of a better cause – why is it that the days fly so swiftly by?" She prefers Lini to Anita but wants to look Enrico in the eye to know whether he is really all right. Probably not. To avoid upset, to get ahead, one has to be like everyone else. That, anyway, is her policy; and when the racial laws are introduced in '38, she sends him recipes for asparagus and *matalviz*, and enquires whether he still has one trouser-leg longer than the other, like the last time they met. Enrico's reply is evasive. That expression "to get ahead" annoys him.

Emma writes most often about her grandson Carlo, Paula's boy. He and his mother are now living in the Dolomites near the Marmolada glacier. Paula's marriage is not going too well, but the Marmolada gleams majestically white, and Carlo is having fun throwing snowballs. From the photo he seems a good-looking lad – full of smiles. It's wrong, she knows, to be seduced by good looks – there's great injustice in charm and good health – but the old woman can't help looking at that photograph. Were she younger, she would make the trip out to Salvore. But seeing each other again is not all that important. "Our bonds, Rico, are the sort that cannot be broken." Enrico knows that she would welcome longer replies from him, but

81

letter-writing is a form of literature, and so he scorns it – preferring by far to make notes on specific uses of *quominus*.

Biagio Marin visits him now and then, and tries to convince him to plant one rose bush at least in front of the house to keep Lini happy. Even if he has never forgotten that morning at school when Carlo took off his round Spanish hat, placed his face and mouth under the fountain, and drank, Biagio can never understand Carlo. For Biagio loves falling water, descending weight, flowing life – loves a life full of both greed and hunger, a life that changes and dissolves continually. As a poet he is capable of seeing God only in the sensual and the finite – things that always become something else: pitchers for drinking, mouths for kissing, greedy idols chanting the eternal psalm of their own intoxicating disappearance.

Enrico thinks of the light Carlo saw where others see only darkness; of seas without shores and furrowed by no keel; of a sun which, on such a sea, never alters and never sets; of a heaven inhabited not by Homer's gods but by Plato's ideal forms. But sometimes that blazing, blinding heaven goes black; he shuts his eyes and plunges into the darkness behind his eyelids. The blazing light scorches and withers. Why choose him of all people? There is need of a stronger tree, one richer in sap and resin, one that can receive the light of the lamp without being burned. He envies Marin, for he has not been struck down by the light and, instead, encounters the eternal in fugitive divinities wherever he looks. Marin nevertheless bears within him the inextinguishable memory of that morning beside the fountain. "We can neither ignore nor forget each other," Enrico writes to him, even though – in a later letter to Paula – he disparages Biagio's limited understanding. For Biagio loves the world, while "Carlo is a saint, detached from this world, in search of another undisturbed by madness and pain".

On some afternoons they visit the Battilanas, whose house, like the couple themselves, is bright and welcoming. They play the piano – Schubert and Beethoven – as did Argia, by that same sea. In a lighter mood, Lidia sings *La Paloma* and Lini plays the zither, its straying tones suiting her austere expression. Enrico smiles and she smiles back, forgetting how he shoved her out of bed and hurt her, remembering instead some of his letters that ended with a kiss. For a moment, sadness vanishes from her eyes, like a light that is extinguished. But the zither has its limits, its sound trails off mutely as huge clouds pass across the heavens, the earth revolves, and coffee and sugar become ever more scarce. Lini's mouth sets bitter again, though *pelinkovec* and *grappa*, fortunately, remain in plentiful supply.

Enrico develops an abscess on his neck. At first he pays it no attention but, as it grows larger, he makes up his mind to act and summons Janes; for he is afraid of illness but even more so of doctors. I didn't think you'd come, he says, as Janes bends over him. I'm here in my professional capacity, comes the reply, although, as he prepares to make the small incision, Janes does not meet Enrico's eye. Janes returns to Valdoltra, where he is compelled by the difficult times to sell part of his house. Skin cancer breaks out on his face, devouring it just as flames shrivel and strip away the covers of old books thrown on the fire. Enrico is sure that he will commit suicide. Instead he dies little by little, like a mushroom attacked by a slow-spreading but relentless mould. Towards the end, thankfully, the process speeds up, and Anita, beautiful but shattered by fatigue, moves to Trieste.

Enrico continues to go out in his boat – often with Pepi, a local fisherman, a willing companion on days of dead-calm, sluggish seas. Enrico keeps among his papers a postcard Pepi sends him from Leipzig. In '39 Paula pays a visit. On gazing into her dark eyes he can believe that the world is not just one awful mistake.

War comes and, like an echo, passes by – or rather, hangs over them oppressively. Enrico keeps abreast of events only indirectly, by hearing of the departure, return, or failure to return of young men of the village whom he does not know. Lia sends him the odd parcel, the Busdachins work the land, and even he, Enrico, feels compelled to read the papers more frequently than before. Luckily the sea does not change, and he can still see from his boat shadows of fish in the depths. In the winter of '41 the *bora* is particularly icy, and Enrico remembers Janes with gratitude, since it was he who had persuaded him to install that stove in the kitchen.

The Germans arrest Carlo's elder sister, Elda. Her mother, now alone, writes to Enrico of her loss of faith in everyone and everything. No one, neither relatives nor friends, shows her any pity; no one has the courage to pay an old Jewess a visit. "You are fortunate, dear Rico, to live far from this nasty, fickle little world." The exterminators' world is small only for an old woman worried about Enrico, fearful that he is too much on his own. "If I were less decrepit," she wrote, "I should come to visit you." And in the next line, she regrets that she lacks her brother's lust for life – he's eighty-six and has just had a nasty accident. Instead, what she is waiting for, she writes, is a peaceful return to that land from which we all have come. "And, dear Rico, talking of land, I imagine you are satisfied with yours and with the wheat that has done well this year."

At Salvore, too, thunderbolts fall in the shape of Germans on motorbikes barking harsh commands like whiplashes in one courtyard after another. Enrico hears tell of an incident at Grubia where a couple of girls were battered to death by the fascists for hiding some partisans, or was it merely some pamphlets? He has never been to Bassanìa, let alone Grubia. Young people and old abandon their homes, and most of the girls are on the move, gathering wood up-country and meeting together at night in some house or other. The Germans spread out, mowing them down as they go. Three youngsters, it is rumoured, were hanged at the roadside near Visignano (others say Pisino) and left there strung up by hooks through their throats. On capture, one of them couldn't utter a word, but the other two yelled "Smrt Fašizmu" and "Živio Tito", raising clenched fists; and one, who knew some German, said something as they hoisted him that made the officer flush with rage, and then tried to spit in his face. It reminds Enrico of the *chilotes* in Patagonia, with the difference that they knew only how to die, while these knew how to kill as well. They say that up on the Neretva river and the Kozara range, the Germans were astounded to find themselves in retreat before a bunch of vagabonds advancing on them out of the woods. Graffiti appear: "Trst je năs"; "It is not Tito who wants Istria, but Istria who wants Tito"; "Život damo Trst ne damo". Some Italian partisans, the report goes, protest about this to the Slavs fighting with them against the Germans and the fascists. They argue that, in the spirit of brotherhood and liberation from tyranny, they shouldn't in their turn become the oppressors and rob the Italians of their rights. But whoever takes this line disappears and ends up at the bottom of a ravine on the Carso, or is captured by the Germans – after being discovered, no one has the faintest idea how, in a secret hide-out.

This too is dumb pain, a weight that falls and crushes, the delirium of believing that life is redeemable, the illusion of the "I" which finds liberation from the world's madness by sinking to the level of brute existence. The tiger believes it is right to devour the antelope. Fortunately life is a short, painful negative adverb – μὴ ὄν – "non-being", and not something everlasting. The eternal scorches that "non", that tiny, ferocious sting. To keep to oneself and to turn to flame – that is true liberation from every single changeable thing. And nothing is more changeable than man.

Graffiti are the lies of those who believe victory is within their grasp. Yet it is equally wrong to deny the Slavs any share in Istria's red land. Contempt, like spit, ultimately falls back on the spitter. More news arrives: near Albona in the heart of the battle, the Titoists have been hurling Italians, guilty or innocent, their hands bound with wire, into the ravines or the sea. Another bubonic plague is breaking out in history. If only they could go back in time to their school desks, to discuss the suppressed tensions that are now exploding; if only Carlo had learned Slovenian; perhaps... who knows... But it's no use putting back the clock: everything would turn out just the same – the same mistakes, the same atrocities.

The Germans have deported Emma and Elda to Auschwitz, but Paula is in Switzerland. A spiritualist neighbour had told them not to worry, that she had contacted Carlo who had communicated by knocking on the table to say that they could safely stay where they were. Emma dies in '43, soon after arrival at the concentration camp, and Elda dies a year later. Both Carlo and Gino his brother killed themselves in their prime, the ancient pain of their race engendering in them an incurable rupture. But it took Auschwitz and the whole *mise-en-scène* of the Third Reich to do away with an 89-year-old Jewess. It is precisely the Thousand-year Reich that proves rhetoric's destructive power. Yes, Enrico repeats to himself and writes to Paula and some other friends, Carlo was supreme; his sun shines brighter and radiates further than even those of Parmenides and Plato. Merely the report of all this tragedy and atrocity serves to make Carlo's name, albeit suppressed and twisted, re-echo in Enrico's ears.

Argia too, though not a Jew, dies in a concentration camp, for she refused to turn a blind eye and spoke out against the Nazi deportations. It was thought that she had been helping

87

the partisans as well. Someone suggests to Enrico that it was her memory of Carlo that made Argia speak and act so fearlessly. Enrico says nothing. His face darkens and he gazes at the pines and Salvore's deserted shore. With whom can he converse among these rocks? He thinks uneasily of Paula's dark eyes. Perhaps it would be better never to see her again.

Tito's ninth armoured division reaches Trieste, entering the city on 1st May 1945, one week before the liberation of Zagreb. Communism's red flag, and the national white, red and blue, cover the heavens like a scarlet cloud; and in the coppery light the reaper's scythe swings indiscriminately. The Triestine Slavs' recovery after their long obscurity breeds its own dark and spreading violence: with the supporters of Tito in power at Gorizia, many, including Nino's widow, Pina, are arrested and never return.

Even Enrico and Captain Pelizzon are arrested and taken to Umago. Sharing the same crowded cell with so many others is intolerable enough. Sweat's fetid stench pervades the airless room – not the sweat of a summer's day or of honest work, but the acid sweat of fear. Not to fear death and not to fear its companion, the fear of death – but the life of persuasion is difficult in practice. It is not easy to tolerate the stench, the interrogations, the beatings; it is hard not to hope at every moment that they will cease, open the door, and let one leave. Here, inside, you would have to be a saint: only saints fear nothing. But Enrico never asked for sainthood or required it of anyone else – not even of Carlo. His only desire in that attic had been to enjoy himself in the company of friends.

Enrico is afraid, but he has a stubborn streak. He is unable to concentrate on the example of Socrates, but he is also incapable of controlling his temper. He scornfully dismisses the soup, telling his gaolers to offer it to those swine of a secret police, even though it's better than the muck they're usually fed in their sties. And when they menace him with their stupid questions, he becomes angry and offensive, firing off insults in Italian and Slovenian, treating them like curs driven from their master's table. They in turn lose their patience – with drastic effect.

It's a curious experience being beaten. But not just curious. There's the pain too and, worse, the sense of helplessness and loss beneath the blows. How insensitive he has been in his intolerance of children! They must often feel as he does now. He tries to think back to when he was a child, but to no avail. Recollection, while trying to shield head and belly, does not come easily.

Enrico has never been in a fist-fight, let alone been beaten up. Such physical, violent closeness utterly bewilders him. A gun battle would be less frightening. Danger he has confronted before – in Patagonia or on the sea – but never anything like this. The world, vast, overwhelming, crushing, is falling in on him. He could never stand people touching him or even taking his arm in conversation. And now this. It hurts, hurts a lot; and it's the indecent intimacy that hurts most. For he's always been one to keep his distance, never wanting to sleep the night with anyone, always choosing separate beds. Even if there were only one, evenly-matched, aggressor out on the pampas, still he would have no notion of self-defence, but would curl up piti-fully and cover his head, like a child hiding beneath the blankets.

It doesn't last long, for they realize their blunder soon enough. A couple of local farmers, who are Party members, explain to police headquarters that "the teacher" is a harmless eccentric, has never been a fascist or even a nationalist, and has never caused any trouble or made any demands. They add that he even knows Slovenian, though he would do better to learn Croat. So they let him go and even apologize. A captain from Zagreb, a fluent Italian-speaker, takes him home to Salvore by car and tells him that now the revolution has come, mistakes like this should never happen again. Enrico doesn't say a word. This is not the moment to express his views on revolution and counter-revolution, or to say what he thinks of all those who are impatient to usher in the future.

Pelizzon is freed too and obtains the right to emigrate. He leaves everything behind and goes to Trieste as an exile, where he gets a council job – the Captain's moment to go ashore has finally arrived. Enrico too is free to leave. But to go where? A city? Trieste is full of cars and turmoil, Gorizia lies too far inland, where shoes are obligatory. Lini becomes rather abrupt and turns more heavily to drink while waiting silently for him to make up his mind.

He stays – to general admiration. But it is fear not courage – fear of staying put, and an even greater fear of leaving. Enrico is no hero. Carlo could have been one, but a hero has to win, and victories are nothing more than tricks and tragedies designed to manipulate the emotions of an audience, an opponent, or a judge. So Carlo declined the part. Heroes and victories are only play-acting. How can you deny the palm of victory to someone who would otherwise make a scene? Indeed, Philoctetes loses. Without the opportunity to show off his strength and sensitivity, he has only his putrid wound for company.

Enrico is afraid – not of people, but of papers, documents, statements, census forms, declarations that he must continually sign, and of taxes too. The agrarian reform confiscates half his land in favour of the tenants. The Busdachins are now landowners and neighbours. Not that he is angry with them personally – had it not been them, it would have been someone else. They are upright folk, after all, and there's no denying they have worked hard all these years. What he detests is communism itself. Conditions are even tougher now, and it is hard to live off the little land he's got left. A vague threat hangs in the air, and even his walks along the beach are clouded in uncertainty. "That teacher who's stayed on at Punta Salvore with a noose around his neck," as a Milanese friend of Bruno Battilana described him in a letter.

Life on this side of the iron curtain is quite a burden. "Dear Biagio, if things persist as they are at present, I shan't hold out much longer. The annulment of individuality is so complete that the slightest activity is frowned upon. Which explains why I can't write in more detail." No letters, no decisions, no hurry; to rest at peace, quiet, immobile – like an oak – looking out to sea. "Dear Paula, everyone is leaving. I haven't made up my mind – there's no rush yet. What concerns me most is never to forsake the sea." Punta Salvore too becomes part of a game whose players are not so much Italy and Yugoslavia, but the distant superpowers. Not having read *Persuasion and Rhetoric*, they believe they can dispute the mastery of the world. Frontiers are re-drawn, lengthened, shortened – on sheets of paper that diplomats exchange with each other before discarding them. Were it not for Lia and the Battilanas, who lend him money and help out when and as they can, it would be difficult for him and Lini to keep going. Even his boat, *Maia*, has been confiscated.

One day Toio Zorzenon stops by with his wife and two small children. A labourer in the shipyards at Monfalcone, he was among the first organizers of the Communist Party's secret cells at the factory. Imprisoned by the fascists and deported by the Germans, he met Busdachin when a partisan in Istria, after his escape from Germany. Despite being Italian, he wants Trieste and the Free Territory to become part of communist Yugoslavia. For in the proletarian revolution national differences count little compared with redemption of the world and its people. However, such ideas brought the nationalists at Monfalcone down on him as well.

He wants to live in Yugoslavia, to help build socialism. A country ruined by war needs trained workers. Some two thousand men from Monfalcone share his views and cross over against the tide of another three hundred thousand Italians who, at different times, pour into Italy from Istria, Fiume, and Dalmatia. Both groups abandon their houses, their roots, everything. Zorzenon has stopped to see Busdachin on his way to work in the mines of the Arsa region. His wife looks lost and doesn't say a word, their children sit on the one or two suitcases they have brought with them. Zorzenon speaks of socialism and the future. Enrico goes off for his walk, to listen to the sound of the sea, while Lini finds a bit of fruit for the children.

"Dearest Biagio, for many years now I have been incapable of living life as I should..." However, when his nephew Gregorio and family come to visit him, he is as abrupt and as obstinate as ever. He is happy enough to see them, but he obliges them to park their car elsewhere, out of sight; and they have to remove their watches, at least when they're with him. Then he starts criticizing Tito and his regime. He doesn't care if those two from the *Milicija* next door hear him or not – he even raises his voice: the Slavs will have to wait a thousand years to take over from Venice. Perhaps by then they will have learned a thing or two. But as long as the communists are still around the Slavs will be cultural pygmies. Gregorio and his wife look around anxiously, but the two militiamen pretend not to hear – they know him only too well. Instead they laugh to each other like schoolboys, taking care the teacher doesn't notice.

In this period, especially in the evenings, Enrico often goes for a stroll along the beach with Battilana. Erect, lean, white hair ever longer and ruffled by the wind, eyes seemingly ever bluer and ever clearer – Enrico speaks of Carlo, and speaks at length, gesturing at the sea. Battilana listens in silence, one step behind. "Who better than Rico to introduce me, a meek and lowly man, to the miraculous force of his twenty-year-old friend? Flashes of love, thunder claps of indomitable will to become One, as God."

Yet Enrico often dries up in mid-sentence. Something chokes inside when Battilana looks at him as he used to look at Carlo. To gather oneself into a single point, to become flame, to be master of oneself with persuasion... If only they would leave him in peace to watch the boys and girls playing ball on the beach. One girl with an angry mouth and long legs kicks the ball into the water where it bobs up and down on the waves, ever in the same place.

Enrico turns back. He speaks little to Lini and does not reply to Biagio's letters and poems. Or if he does, he scribbles a couple of lines at most – to justify his silence. Even with Gaetano he writes only to make excuses. He doesn't react to Lisetta's letter describing her life at Danzig with her husband and her two little daughters when the Reich collapsed, how the Russians invaded, of her escape with the children in a torrent of refugees. He writes resentfully to Lia telling her to pay him for her side of the apartment which they own jointly. True, her section is much bigger, and yes she has paid for it, but, as he points out, she inherited the money from her father – and therefore from his mother – her father was his mother's darling, the only one she cared about – she had no time for that other son in Patagonia. And even if Lia has put some of her own money towards it, that's no concern of his: she must do as he says. If everyone believes that they have a right to their own opinion, even ignoramuses who know no Greek, the world will be in real trouble.

Lia not only lets him say his piece, she also posts him some parcels and money, in excess, even, of his share in the

94

apartment. Enrico sends her a receipt and scrawls a bad-tempered letter of thanks. Women like Lia and the Busdachin woman, with their liberal open-handedness – which you can't help noticing even in the way they serve you at table – make him feel distinctly shabby. But they are all just a gaggle of silly geese, they don't realize that only megalomaniacs go in for grand gestures.

Chiavacci is working on a new edition of Carlo's collected works. "Dearest Gaetano, be happy in the knowledge that you are capable of the task... Your name and Arangio's will be coupled with His; and in time posterity will realize that he is the greatest figure Europe has ever produced." Enrico cares little that his own name is not linked with Carlo. On the contrary – it is better that it should be erased. He is fortunate not to have the ability of either Chiavacci or Arangio-Ruiz. Enrico writes to Gaetano about his own inability – with a certain false modesty – and then crosses out what he has said with a single thin line that leaves the words clearly visible. Carlo is the Buddha of the western world. That is enough. When the journal, *La fiera letteraria*, remembers him and asks for a contribution to an issue devoted to Michelstaedter, Enrico sends them a short paragraph, which is published along with the full and discursive essays written by many others, only to say that Carlo and Buddha are the two great awakened ones, of West and East respectively.

To dim, to dull the perceptible, as did Buddha, and not to notice that mutability of things which so pleases Biagio. He meets Zorzenon's wife again, at her wits' end, exhausted and terrified, traipsing from prison to consulate to embassy the length and breadth of Yugoslavia. Toio is confined on Goli Otok, the barren island where Tito has set up a concentration camp for Stalinists. She tells her story in a voice more exhausted than anxious. Yet she can never tell it right through, she keeps going back to the beginning, she interrupts and repeats herself. She tells how, when Tito broke with Stalin, the communists from Monfalcone protested and then ended up along with Croat fascists and common criminals on Goli Otok and Sveti Grgur, two islands of the northern Adriatic that had been turned into prison camps like those some of them knew in Germany – or even like those in the Soviet Union, that are known to exist despite the official silence and the discounting of any shred of evidence as slanderous fantasy. The community of evil, as Enrico knows, is alive and well.

The woman describes Goli Otok. Her murmuring words flow like water, harmless, even caressing at first hearing, but containing tales of horror. So it is that books – all books – are easy, while people and things are difficult. Forced labour in freezing conditions, beatings, deaths, heads thrust into cesspits, and worst of all the *bojkot* – when the comrade who obstinately refuses to submit is mercilessly battered by his fellow prisoners hopeful of improving their own conditions.

Toio's wife has received no definite news for some time now – not even to know whether he is dead or alive. She goes to one office after another, writes to consulates and ministries, but no one can give her any information. She is sent from pillar to post in Yugoslavia; in Italy they don't know where even Istria

96

is, let alone the whereabouts of two small islands. And when they finally grasp something of the story, they smile complacently and joke that it will do the communists good to learn what communism is really about; while the English and Americans do not even want to listen to anyone who is pro-Stalin and anti-Tito. And the communist newspapers, although they rage against the Yugoslav revisionists, never mention concentration camps and forced labour.

She is penniless and, like countless other women in the same boat, receives no financial help for the children. Some Croatian families give them food and a place to sleep when they can, while Toio – if he is still alive – and the others battle on in the Lager in Stalin's name, refusing to submit.

She leaves for Zagreb and the Superintendent of the prisons. They give her a few slices of ham and some fruit. This is the life, rich in its changing scenes, that appeals to the poets and bards of myths and metamorphoses. Enrico closes his eyes: he wants to transcend earthly perception like Buddha. To be awoken signifies precisely that – sleep. Even the waves' reflection hurts the eyes. The sea surrounding the hell of Goli Otok is as enchanting as it is cruel. What else can one expect from the perfidious sea?

"Dear Paula, 17th October is drawing near. With every passing year I perceive Carlo's greatness ever more clearly... year after year I feel closer to him, the perfect saint and sage." Paula lends Enrico money for which, as for anything that binds him to her, he is both happy and grateful. The only time he entertains the idea, even if only fleetingly, of leaving Salvore, is when he hears that there is a cottage available near hers at Cormons in the Collio mountains.

Have they not perhaps always lived together? It is now almost seventeen years since their last meeting. And the number of times they have met since those three days together at Pirano and Salvore in 1909 can be counted on the fingers of one hand. But what does it matter if branches grow apart, provided that the same sap flows through them? "I wish for both of us," he wrote, "that our hopes (which are more or less identical) are not disappointed in the New Year, as so often in the past. But as long as our wishes are united it makes little difference if they remain unfulfilled."

He does not go to visit Paula. His pass has expired and he would have to submit to too many bureaucratic procedures to renew it: applications, stamps, even a photograph. He asks her to go to Carlo's grave for him on 17th October, and to place there in his name, as Signora Emma used to do, violets wreathed in the yellow horse-chestnut leaves from Piazza Ginnastica – where he and Carlo used to go after school.

Instead, Paula comes to visit him on his birthday, 1st June 1956. What are seventy years? Carlo is twenty-three, Paula seventy-one. How old are those dark eyes? Lini prepares something to eat. The sea sparkles beyond the pines, they feel the wind on their faces. Paula bends down, picks up a pine cone and throws it at a tree; she misses and laughs. If only that moment could last for eternity, that laugh without future, that pine cone, and that brown spot on the hand that holds it – the imprint of the passing years – intimacy and trembling, familiarity hesitant to take that hand, for nothing after all has happened, and their life has been spent together. Paula comes back twice more. Twice is a lot, like those three full days at Pirano and Salvore.

He must really go to Gorizia, to the cemetery. He does not now require a pass, since the tomb is situated in the Yugoslav section, in Nova Gorica. But there is no hurry. People want to do everything in a hurry. One day he will also go to Bassanìa, but right now he needs peace. Travel means organization, deciding on dates and times, finding out about buses. Recently he has been even more reluctant than usual to sort things out, happy enough to let himself be pushed this way and that by conflicting and confused messages on all sides. He dates a letter to Gaetano as 20th (*circa*) May, since in that moment he can neither remember what day it is nor be bothered to find out. No matter if it's actually the 23rd.

Someone, he can no longer remember who, has urged him to write his memoirs. But he is not keen on the idea. His memories are his own property. It is madness to give them away to others, like Tolstoy's idea of giving everything to the poor. Besides, even if he wanted to write his memoirs, how could he? One needs peace and quiet, the certainty that no one is going to come and knock on the door. True – Punta Salvore, compared to elsewhere, is a serene haven. But even here you can't be sure that you'll have no callers. To write, you have to be sure.

He now spends even more time walking by the cliffs. For when people ask him something, even Lini, he either does not understand them or, just as he is about to reply, he can no longer remember the original question. It is better so. He has no difficulty understanding the cries of the seagulls. As always he goes around without shoes, and he must have become more resistant to cold, since he puts nothing over his summer shirt even when an icy *bora* is blowing – though, admittedly, he does feel better when Lini pushes a woollen jumper over his head and arms. He spends even longer, sometimes hours on end, gazing at the sea. Catching sight of sea urchins in the shallows he thrusts his hand in to the water and pulls them out. Despite wounding himself on their spines, he straight away forgets the pain and plucks at them afresh.

Talk turns to Toio. A woman from Salvore, who has been to Trieste, has seen his wife. He and the others were liberated a few years ago and returned to Monfalcone, where he discovered that his house had been taken by refugees from Yugoslavia. People now treat him as a Titoist who betrayed his country. Not even the Communist Party wants to know, for it is people like him who remind the Party of what it prefers to forget, namely the Stalinist movement against Tito. Perhaps, his wife said, they might emigrate to Australia. Enrico listens, but without understanding anything or remembering who this Toio person is.

He is happier than ever. The world around him is tranquil at last. After the storm the breakers have now ceased their furious crashing on the shore, the roaring has stilled to a whispering backwash. Everything grows quiet, which is good. Sometimes as he stoops inside the caves along the beach he loses his balance, stumbles, and has to lean against the rock wall. Once he loses his way home: he must have gone further than he thought; perhaps he has finally reached Bassanìa. Then a woman with broad flanks and open smiling eyes half-buried in the deep-set lines of her peasant skin takes him by the arm. He recognizes her but cannot for the moment recall her name. After a few minutes he finds himself at home.

Paula comes to visit him and finds him on the beach steadying himself on Lini's arm, staring at the waves colliding as they wash in and out. It is late, already November 1959. Enrico speaks in monosyllables, repeatedly shaking his head. Paula leans against a tree, just as she leaned against a chest of drawers on that 17th October when she heard about Carlo.

Now in the strip of pines by the beach workmen are installing campsite facilities. They work hard and stake out the land, but they're a bunch of amateurs and keep forgetting their wooden pegs in the ground. Enrico stops and struggles to pull them out. The men have no idea: they take the pegs from him and put them back again – in the wrong place as before. But they are polite at least and escort him home. He wants to explain that they've got it wrong but finds himself mumbling and becoming flustered – it must be because he doesn't speak Croat.

With Lini too he speaks little. But no matter. She undresses him, puts him to bed, lies down and embraces him for a while. The scent of her skin, dry and pungent like a wild flower, that has always pleased him, reminds him vaguely of something he can't quite place, and he gropes towards her before letting his hand fall back upon the sheets. Lini caresses him and goes to her own bed.

They admit him to hospital at Capodistria. While there he recognizes no one, and after a few days they send him home again. As they are helping him from the ambulance, the Busdachin woman, who is supporting him, notices how he raises his eyes to look around: the red earth, the pine tops, the sea beyond. Just for a moment a smile, or so it seems, plays upon his motionless lips. They put him to bed and leave him alone. Lini knows he wants it that way. She leaves the room, looking at him as she closes the door.

Enrico lies there, his eyes fixed on a stained and cracked corner of the wall. Illuminated by Carlo's lamp the stain at first grows bigger and more discoloured, and then shrinks – a fish-scale, an island, the rapacious eye of a *cimango*, a nipple, a scattered handful of sand, ink that flicks on to the faded grey of the classroom. The crack in the ceiling near the portrait of Schopenhauer gapes, the light flickers to and fro making the wall tremble. Nino moves the lamp, Carlo's eyes glow in the shadows and sink into dark-brown waters, Paula lifts her eyelashes, the sea spreads on all sides, one knee hurts, but only slightly, and then the pain subsides. The lamp's oil overflows. The body is a balloon that a child inflates with all his breath. It lights up inside, grows and fills the whole sphere of the heavens with a clear, steady, even glow. There is nothing more – no one to hear the gentle bursting as a pine needle punctures the balloon or the welling up of the oil as it bubbles over to choke the flame.

102

The rest of the story following that 5th December 1959 is briefly told. Lini keeps watch alone over Enrico all night long. It is not much different from many recent vigils. She gazes at him earnestly but without tears, every so often taking his hand in hers. She buries him in the cemetery at Salvore and continues to live in the house. Fourteen years slip by, one inside the other like the Chinese boxes she played with as a child. Wine and *pelinkovec* rinse the years of their colour, leaving them opaque, and on some days morning and afternoon are indistinguishable. Compared with Carlo I meant nothing to him, she tells visiting nephews and nieces. In her relations with the Busdachins she is often brusque or unresponsive, although on some evenings she sits with the old woman beneath the olive trees. She finds peace in that broad face with its kind, quizzical look.

Paula dies in 1972. She wrote that Rico's death caused her less distress than did their last meeting. When they find Lini at the foot of the stairs on 3rd December 1973, she has been dead for several hours. She must have fallen from the top landing, where the drinks cupboard is located, and fractured her skull. After the funeral her relatives gather together a few books and papers, including Tolstoy's letter, and lock everything else, books, pamphlets, and all odd sheets of paper in the large studded trunk by the window. Lia gives the lamp to her daughter Anna who lives at Gorizia, where she is married to one Luzzatto, a relative of Carlo's mother.

Ten years afterwards, a new critical edition of the works of Michelstaedter is published and, because of its scholarly rigour and completeness, it becomes the definitive text. A note in the *Epistolario*, later reprinted in a number of other publications, anticipates the passing of Enrico Mreule by twenty-six years, supposing him to have died at Umago in 1933.